THE PSYCHOPATH

Other Maguire Crime books:

Murder by the Bottle by Ed Whitfield

THE PSYCHOPATH

ACADEMIC
HUSBAND
FATHER
SERIAL KILLER

A M EDWARDS

MAGUIRE
CRIME

Published by Maguire Crime
an imprint of RedDoor Press
www.reddoorpress.co.uk

The author and publisher gratefully acknowledge permissions granted to
reproduce the copyright material in this book
p 84 'Soft As Your Face' words and music by Sean Dickson
© Big Life Publishing. Reproduced with permission

P 172 'Meaner Than Mean' words and music by Malcolm Treece, Martin
Gilks, Miles Hunt, Robert Jones
© Universal Music Publishing 1988. Reproduced with permission of Hal
Leonard Europe Ltd.

P 232 'Male Stripper' words and music by Miki Zone.
© Paul Zone Cilione. Published by Paul Zone Music

ISBN 978-1-913062-84-2

A CIP catalogue record for this book is available from the British Library

Typesetting: Jen Parker, Fuzzy Flamingo
www.fuzzyflamingo.co.uk

Printed and bound in Denmark by Nørhaven

Cover design: Rawshock Design

This book is dedicated to everyone on my list

The Present Tale

Autumn, 2019

I press Don Chaucer's polyester sweater to the dampness of the floor, but it's proving particularly ineffective as a sponge. As a university vice-chancellor he could undoubtedly have afforded better quality clothing. How proud he was to be in charge at Francis Drake University in Carlisle, bless him. It was his first proper leadership role too; I almost feel guilty for killing him. It'd been a while since I worked with him at Drake's, so today must have come as a surprise.

I finish mopping the small puddle of urine he deposited on the carpet as I suffocated him. A woollen sweater would have worked better, I think, but as I finish my task, my mind drifts to a philosophical argument. What exactly is the difference between a psychopath and a sociopath?

Strictly speaking, both terms are shorthand references to antisocial personality disorders. I tried to look up their differences once using an online dictionary, the type I strongly disapprove of my students using. Although the terms are apparently often misused, both psychopaths and sociopaths evidently lack remorse, empathy, and have a total disregard for morals and/or the law. So, either seems to fit me well, even if only superficially. Being superficial is also how I manage to blend into polite society so elegantly, even to the extent that I currently hold a highly respectable job as pro-vice-chancellor for research at the University of South Lancashire in Ormskirk (USL).

After failing to satisfy my curiosity with online search engines, I decided to further investigate the traits of these antisocial conditions using more robust sources. One rather good narrative review from a prominent psychiatrist suggested sociopaths tend to form emotional connections better than psychopaths, or at least psychopaths find this a more difficult skill to master. The review stated:

'Psychopaths are a more intelligent kind of antisocial, better at hiding their true personality.' Or so Dr Henning of Oxford said in her paper.

This seemed a reasonable observation which I imagine to be correct as a psychopath's true nature is probably the more terrible, although I suspect being a psychopath does not necessarily mean you're a killer. Unlike me of course, and I've hidden my true nature for years. I would never voluntarily come forward to reveal it, not even to those closest to me. But after my background reading, I was still not definitively sure where I fit in, although I do like Dr Henning's view of psychopaths being more intelligent than sociopaths. I clearly self-identify as a psychopath because being more intelligent appeals to my academic vanity, although it seems hard on sociopaths if they are considered the intellectually inferior relation to more sophisticated psychopaths. But vanity aside, what makes me think I'm a psychopath and not a sociopath? I suppose being a psychopath sounds more menacing, deadlier, and perhaps a bit sexier. I mean, if you're going to be bad you might as well go all the way, and being a psychopath sounds very bad. From a practical perspective, I must also ask whether or not your average social-climbing sociopath would be in my position now with a dead body lying next to them? I think not. I am a badge-carrying, serial-killing psychopath and proud of it.

The Tale of the Bank

Winter, 1990

I have rapidly come to the conclusion that working for a high street bank was a particularly poor career choice. 'Jez, you need a job,' Dad had said. I think he just wanted some rent money to buy booze. It's my first proper job since completing A levels last summer and I have to say this career is not turning out to be as exciting as it seemed in the brochure.

The branch where I work is in the small market town of Abingdon. We're central to the local community and most people know one another here. If I were uncharitable, I would also say they're probably all related in one way or another. Some of the girls are pretty enough but mostly they are short with fat ankles. If you look too closely, almost everyone has some flaw or other, nothing so bad as having a third ear or anything like that, but enough to make you think there's something genetically wrong somewhere. I shouldn't want to contribute to the problem, although as I'm six foot four inches tall, lean, and I think quite handsome, I might even out the genes a bit better. Ideally, I should have moved from the area when I had the chance and gone straight to university, but for better or worse, I made the decision to stay. I thought building a career in banking was a good move, but it's incredibly dull.

Our bank building is Edwardian style: tall, elegant and smart, yet severe. It's also always very cold. While that's not a good thing, at least the low temperature makes women's nipples erect when they've been in here a while. Observing the female form is one of the few things that make it passable to get through the day; that and the regular visits to my cashier's desk from jockeys of the nearby racing stables. They come in to cash their salaries every week and then immediately spend it all at the local pub, or illegally betting on each other's races. At least occasionally they give the cashiers some betting tips. Some of the jockeys are more reliable than others and as I've learnt, it's best to stay away from the ones smelling of alcohol at 10 a.m. There are a few of those who nervously wait for us to check their account balances before we hand over any money. I think they hope by giving us tips we will establish some camaraderie. But the career of a junior bank clerk would not last long if you start giving out cash to people who have nothing in their account.

It's 9.05 a.m. on Monday morning and Lindsey the head cashier passes me a handwritten note as I attend to the early influx of morning customers, all those with the same idea to trying avoid a queue meaning they then end up causing one. When the initial rush is over, I read it:

Jez. Leighton has asked if you could come upstairs to see him.

I swivel round on my cashier's stool to face Lindsey, while I still hold the note. I notice with disappointment she's wearing a heavy sweater today. She catches my eye as I look at her.

'What now?' I ask with some trepidation, waving the note at her. Apart from the jockeys and checking out women, the most interesting role here is working as a cashier because you get to handle all the money. My rotation on the counter has lasted a while and I hope it will continue. Mostly the senior managers leave you alone to get on with it as they don't want you to make any errors. Errors in cashing up at the end of the day mean everyone must stay late, and no one wants that. So an interruption like this from the assistant branch manager is not what's needed as it could throw me off. This is particularly the case when he is widely known to be an asshole. Lindsey shrugs at me with a maternal smile. She'd make a much better assistant branch manager.

'I think he wants you to go straight up when you get a moment. I'll cover your counter until you get back.' I sigh and then log myself off. As I pass her, I notice she looks pensive. Pensive and yet hot.

Seeing Leighton is not something I've done much, other than to say hello when I first joined the bank a while ago, but obviously I've heard of his reputation. The assistant branch manager is much like a school's deputy head and runs the place, or at least thinks he does. Leighton is by no means an attractive man; he's short and squat, in his mid-thirties, a wearer of oversized aviator-style spectacles, has the puffy jawline of a committed non-exerciser, curly receding hair and he wears suits that look like they have been ironed too often.

'OK, I'll go now then,' I say and Lindsey pats me on the shoulder like she might do to someone heading for the gallows. I don't like it much – unsolicited touching is not something I am too comfortable with, even from a sexy older woman with nice breasts, albeit inconveniently concealed from the cold weather today under her sweater. There's a general silence in the rest of the room among my ten or so colleagues in the junior clerks' ground floor bullpen. They seem to know something. I'm not being sacked, am I?

'Good luck,' whispers Maxine. She's one of the other juniors – a plain girl but friendly, as plain girls tend to be. I'm not sure why I should need luck.

I walk slowly up the winding staircase, across the first floor filled by the investments team, and knock on his door.

'Come,' he says gruffly. I enter his office cautiously as he doesn't sound jovial. Leighton barely looks up at me, which I think is rather rude. I'm twice the size of him and I doubt he would be so abrupt with me outside of the workplace – or if he were, he might not like my reaction. When he does look up, it's not to look at me but to examine something on the microfiche screen on his desk. It's the same style of device I use on the counter to check whether or not people have funds in their accounts.

'I've been examining the staff balances this morning Jeremy and it appears you are overdrawn,' he says, now staring at me. He's calling me Jeremy, that's not good.

'Oh yes?' I ask, feeling caught and sensing myself colouring slightly with embarrassment. I'm usually quite careful with money. 'I'm not sure how that has happened,' I say, stumbling to think what it was I hadn't properly accounted for. He's still looking at me over the top of his glasses and apparently able to do so without blinking. He pauses slightly before responding while clasping his two stubby index fingers together in front of his face in a prayer position.

'It seems you have been writing cheques when you did not have the funds for them in your account,' he says, occasionally now blinking like a frog. I think about it and realise I was fairly close to the mark this last month and I could have made a miscalculation, particularly as I've just bought some exciting home gym equipment. It's not easy staying sleekly muscled and well-dressed while balancing your accounts on a low salary. I try to explain this to him, but he does not display any flicker of empathy. 'You realise it's a criminal offence to write cheques without sufficient funds in your account?' He hasn't blinked again but I acknowledge that I do appreciate his observation.

'I'm so sorry Leighton', I say and assure him it won't happen again.

'It isn't me you should apologise to; it's the bank and our shareholders. How can we expect customers to show financial responsibility if we are not capable of it ourselves?' I nod my agreement to him. I come to the conclusion he is not so nice, but this is part of the job I have been trained to do when serving customers. Always make sure there's sufficient money in the account before sanctioning a withdrawal.

'I'm really sorry, but that was a genuine miscalculation,' I say and hope it will be the end of the matter, but he still doesn't look happy. 'I can immediately move some money into that account,' I add. 'How much are we talking?'

'Three pounds in deficit and of course there is the ten pounds unauthorised overdraft fee on top of that,' he says. 'We simply cannot have staff of this bank going overdrawn.'

'Three pounds?' I ask. He nods earnestly. I bite my tongue knowing it's only two days until our monthly salaries are due to be deposited into staff accounts. His gaze remains fixed on me for far too long. After further grilling for another ten minutes, I close his door behind me and let out a large sigh. I feel severe dislike building inside me. I walk towards the stairs reflecting that I have never quite known anything like the dressing down I've just had. It feels like I've been violated. At one stage of our meeting, he'd proudly produced a file compiled on me of all my bank statements over the last twelve months. Then to top it off he phoned my credit card company in front of me to ask them to confirm my latest outstanding balance. It was a complete humiliation and he seemed to revel in it.

I had to confirm I could credit my account with fourteen pounds to return it to credit for the next two days until we are paid. It sounded so childlike when I had to confirm that I would ask my father for the money. I could feel rage building inside and I visualised walking straight back into his office and crashing the stupid microfiche machine over his head.

'How did it go?' asks Maxine as I walk back past her desk. I shrug, trying not to show my anger, although I see it's nice of her to ask. I lower my head, avoid further eye contact with her or anyone else and make my way back to the counter.

The Present Tale

A noise is coming closer along the corridor outside the vice-chancellor's office and I freeze to the spot trying to recognise it. My buttock cheeks clench as I perch, resting myself on the edge of his desk. I tighten my fist around the disposable pen I'm holding, thinking fast about how I could use it as a weapon while I visually scan the room for better options. My Taser is out of reach and I haven't recharged it since I fired it into Don's chest an hour ago. Nevertheless, you can do a lot of damage with a pen; I've even seen YouTube clips on it, although it could be messy. The handle of the door turns and I clench the pen harder.

'Not now,' I shout, in a deep, dismissive tone. This is how I recall Don speaking and is the best imitation of him I can manage in the circumstance.

'No problem. Sorry to disturb you Vice-Chancellor,' someone replies. It's an elderly female voice and my grip on the pen loosens slightly as the door handle stops turning. She's no threat to me and I hear the wheels of a trolley now squeaking away into the distance. It's only the cleaning lady.

That was bad timing, but it's useful that I'm a decent mimic of Don. I shudder at the thought of him and as I look down at his corpse on the floor, I give it a casual kick. But this is not the time for such idle pleasure; I have work to do and need to focus on the job in hand, namely what to do with the body of a vice-chancellor from a lowly ranked university once you've killed him.

Although this is a situation I had planned, it was a rushed job. Don's sexual pestering of Bella meant I needed to act and so I know I have been rather hasty, killing him out of jealousy. So I am somewhat outside of my comfort zone today, although the act of killing is obviously a joy at any time. In many ways it's one of life's little pleasures when you get the opportunity to indulge it. I might describe it much like a trip to the spa to get a facial. It's not something I often do, but when I do, I always think I should do it more. But having an unexpected visit from the cleaner confirms my preparations were sloppy today, and imperfections mean consequences and that could be prison. Perhaps my shoddy approach is evidence that I'm a sociopath after all, not a true psychopath or maybe a psychopath of only moderate intelligence. My PhD says otherwise, so I smile for a moment at my cleverness then realise this is not good use of my time, given the pressing situation I'm faced with. So, I slap both my cheeks and give myself a pep talk to sharpen my focus. I'll need to get my act together if I'm to pull this off.

I move close to the door and can hear into the corridor as the cleaner stops after a brief period of vacuuming. That noise is now replaced by humming as she moves further away. What is that tune? I do know it and I'm sure it's from an old TV show, but I can't quite place it. It's really bugging me now and I'm tempted to ask her, but I don't think that would be good for her or me.

I get back on task and as I look around the room surveying whether there is any damage or anything out of place, it hits me like a thunderbolt. I can recall that song after all, which is a relief as in my haste to kill Don I hadn't even considered what would make an appropriate theme song for this happy occasion. Songs are the perfect accompaniment to murder in my experience and I'm working towards my personal top forty. The song is 'White Horses', a great song from a truly terrible, sentimental old TV show. I start to hum it quietly to myself, swaying gently to the rhythm of the music, moving around the room, checking off the scene of my crime, happy in my work.

Don's office is big, in a building that's a bit ugly in a breeze-block, minimalist way, but size-wise it is befitting of a vice-chancellor, even one like him. It has some expensive looking prints on the walls, including a portrait of the first vice-chancellor, Don's grandfather. So I gyrate to the tune of 'White Horses' under his grandfather's picture, seeing my reflection in the glass of the portrait, thinking how handsome I look in this light.

The Tale of the Bank

A few weeks pass at the bank and I have a new homework project to complete for my evening business course. The classes are alright, but after a day of work I find it difficult to concentrate properly and generally I think I'm quite lazy. I know I could do better if I put the effort in, but I'm finding banking and the basic level of these classes a bit too easy.

'The next assignment is a work-based project,' says the tutor as I stuff papers with scrawled notes on them into my Lacoste designer briefcase that cost me a fortune. My heart sinks, as I know who authorises these types of projects at the bank.

'Is there an alternative assessment, like an essay?' I ask. The tutor shakes her head. There's no escaping it, I will have to ask Leighton to approve the project.

As we make our way out of the college, it looks like my classmates are going out for a beer to finish the evening off. I decide to join them.

Standing in the bustle of the busy bar, I'm tapped on the shoulder from someone ahead of me in the queue as I try to push my way into a better position. 'Fancy a beer?' she says. It's Maxine from the office – she's on the course too although I'm not sure how; she seems a bit thick to me. However, she's conveniently placed in the queue, so I nod happily. I gratefully make my way out of the throng and leave her to it. I move back to the calmer seating area and see a spare chair near where Vicky and Clara are sitting. Vicky's chatting about her boyfriend Simon who's taken a year off after finishing his A levels and is travelling the world with a couple of male friends. I know Simon; he's a nice guy, comes from money and likes to sleep around. Vicky doesn't know this, nor that he absolutely didn't want her to go with him. She's blissfully unaware this means he's not that into her and mostly just likes having her hang around for casual sex. I can't blame him, she's a very pretty, petite blonde.

'So I said I'll wait for him,' I hear her say to Clara as I sit down. I think about getting back up again so as not to be drawn into this conversation, but she's cute so I sit down anyway. Clara's nodding sincerely in agreement with her. They're not stupid girls per se, but they really don't know him. I nod in agreement as it seems easier than offering a proper opinion. I'm tired too after a long day and looking at Clara now I conclude that both of them are pretty so I'm more than happy to hang out here for a while if they don't spend the rest of the night talking about Simon.

'You know Simon, don't you Jez? Did he talk to you about his plans?' asks Clara and I internally groan. Vicky's looking at me intensely; she's smiling but it's a smile of desperation and I can see she's trying to hide the desire to shake information from me, needing it, craving it. 'Come on you bastard, tell me everything you know,' that's what she wants to say to me. I can see it in her eyes – what would she do for that information I wonder? She leans in closer to better hear and I instantly become distracted by her pretty face and the slightest sight of her cleavage. Goodness, she's cute – why would he leave her? Maybe she's a bit uptight. From what I know of Simon, he's planning a slow trip around the seedier parts of Asia visiting as many prostitutes as his budget will allow. And he's rich so he could be gone a while.

'Oh, I think he just wants to explore the world a bit,' I say, jauntily. Vicky nods and Clara reclines in her seat.

'See Vicky, I told you,' she says.

'Yes, that's what he told me too. So I said I would wait for him,' Vicky says quickly, nodding. She looks like she's supressing a tear. It's sad really, she'll clearly hang on to the thought of him coming back for the whole of the next year while he's blowing his inheritance in Asian brothels.

'Here you go, Jez,' says a voice over my shoulder. I turn my head and Maxine is waving a pint of beer in my direction. I say beer, but unfortunately she's got me lager. Lager isn't really beer in my vocabulary but it'll do.

'Oh thanks, Maxine,' I say, taking it from her and putting it down on the table in front of me. I'll drink it somehow – maybe when no one is looking. Lager is a chavvy beer for sweaty people with fat bellies who like to shout on football terraces. She hangs around for a while but there isn't room for her to sit down, so she eventually moves off back to the busy bar area where there's another cluster of the junior bankers chatting.

'Jez?' says Clara. I take a discreet sip of my beer and look in her direction. I sense with dread another question coming.

Looking closely at Clara now, she's not quite so attractive as Vicky but is alright, maybe a six out of ten, but with her heavier bosom and a couple of pints in me she could be seven. Vicky is very clearly a solid nine. Both of them work in a nearby branch of the same bank as me so we vaguely know each other from training events and, of course, our evening classes. It's nice to have a bunch of people all around the same age going through the same experiences at work, so a catch-up beer like this is handy even if just to unwind. That is perhaps the only thing I like about being at the bank right now. Apart from checking out women and chatting with the jockeys.

'Yes, Clara?' I say making a fuss of the question as if she has something prophetic to say. She doesn't.

'You do know Maxine likes you, don't you?' she says.

'Does she?' I say. I hadn't realised. She nods and Vicky joins her in laughing; now their smiles look more genuine which lightens the atmosphere. I turn to look towards the bar and see Maxine standing with a bunch of the other bankers sipping a glass of wine, nodding to whatever one of them is saying. She looks over as she sees me and smiles. I nod at her. The two girls see this too and laugh. She could have gotten me a real ale instead of this lager.

'See, I told you,' says Clara.

'You were pretty rude not to talk to her after she got you a drink,' says Vicky. I can't say I thought too much about it or about Maxine at all. Yes she bought me a drink, but it was the wrong one and I did say thank you. She's not really my type; probably a five out of ten – a bit mousey looking.

We only stay for one drink as it's a working day tomorrow, people are tired and we all need to drive home. Nevertheless, a short relax after the stresses of a long day was welcome. I haven't yet bothered to learn how to drive a car so my mode of transport is a low-powered motorbike that sounds like a hairdryer when I over-rev the throttle. I can ride this without having to take a test, which is great. Although it does mean I have to attach annoying learner plates to the bike, which is a bit less cool than I thought it would be when buying it. It also rains a lot in England and I hadn't considered that too much either. All I was thinking was being like Kiefer Sutherland and his gang of motorbike riding vampire teens in the movie *The Lost Boys* that came out a couple of years ago. The cool of balmy California is lost on a wet November day in Abingdon. It's also not ideal to have to wear waterproof trousers over my suit, a heavy leather jacket which makes me sweat, and a helmet which flattens my hair, making a mockery of all the time I spend styling it. It's a purchase I did not properly consider. Also, all my capital is now tied up in the motorbike and I didn't have much to start with. So the damn bike is partly responsible for my finances running so close to the wire and then being bawled out by Leighton.

It's a chilly night as we leave the pub. I zip up my leather biker jacket – it may make me sweat, but at least it's a designer brand. I glance over to Vicky and Clara to see if they notice how expensive it looks, but they're already walking off together to share a ride. I sigh, but thankfully it's not raining so I can try to be a little bit cool, still wearing a helmet but not the full wet weather trousers that make me look ridiculous.

'Off home?' I hear someone say. I turn around with my helmet on as I sit on the bike. Maxine is standing next to me.

'Yes,' I say. I'm not sure if she is a bit simple as clearly that's exactly what I'm doing.

'Can you give me a lift? I've never had a go on a motorbike before,' she says.

'It's not really allowed within the terms of my licence,' I explain. Besides, she obviously doesn't have a helmet.

'Oh, OK,' she says and starts to head off to the crowd in the car park to ask someone else for a lift, but she turns back.

'Don't worry about Leighton,' she calls out. 'He does that to everyone. He's a total bastard.' I give her a half smile, although I had been trying to forget about it. I doubt she can see my smile through the helmet, so I nod too. It's good to know I'm not an isolated case and I have to admit I feel real animosity towards him now. I should try and relieve that somehow – maybe I should take up boxing or something. But then I could be hit in the face and lose a tooth. I spent years wearing braces to have perfect teeth and I don't want them casually knocked out by some thug in the gym. I wave back to her as she smiles and runs off to get a ride.

On my way back home, I think more and more about Leighton. I grip the handlebars of my motorbike more tightly than usual, over-revving the engine as I weave through the dark country lanes. I take cornering more aggressively than normal, which makes me feel edgy, like a vampire teen tearing up the street, maybe even taking off into the air, or as much as you can on a 125CC motorbike.

The Present Tale

I finish dusting all the surfaces and objects I could have touched in Don's office. He has a nice old oak bookshelf filled with ancient-looking periodicals. It gives the place a pseudo-Oxbridge feel without the high achievement. I have my doubts that Don read any of them. He certainly gave me no impression that he was a serious academic when I worked at Drake's. As I smell the books, they have the stench of charity shops about them and I wonder if he bought them in bulk to appear studious.

From the other side of the room there's an excellent view over the central quad where it catches the morning sun. I always liked this room when I was invited to meetings here. From time to time I even allowed myself to dream that I might end up as vice-chancellor at Drake's one day. But then Don arrived and instantly had the look of a man who had won the lottery and Drake's was his prize. He would not give it up voluntarily, but of course that was still no reason to kill the man, at least not yet. But pestering Bella for sex was justifiable as a reason for me and he needed to go. The thought of his scaly old body sweating on top of her was not good. Not that she would have let him, or at least I don't think so.

The Tale of the Bank

Almost a week passes and I haven't mentioned my homework project to Leighton. I can't face the prospect of being stuck in a room with him so I keep putting it off. It's almost lunch time and Lyndsey has just hung up the internal phone. 'Jez, Leighton would like to see you,' she says. I sigh, not again.

'Me?' I ask and feel a rush of heat pass through my cheeks. I can't be overdrawn again.

'Yes, he asks if you're free to come now.'

It's only been a week or so since we were paid. I quickly fire up the microfiche machine to check my balance. I'm relieved to see I still have a couple of hundred pounds in there. It'll still be tight at the end of the month, but I'm healthily enough in credit for now. As long as I don't go out clubbing too much I should be able to make it through to the next pay day.

'Did he say what he wants?' I ask her as I start to close up my counter.

'No, he didn't,' she says. She comes to take over.

It's almost time for my break anyway, so I pack up and let her slip into my place.

'I'll come straight back after my break then,' I say and she nods. She looks solemn, which worries me. I walk slowly upstairs to the management floor but don't see Maxine anywhere along the way to wish me luck this time.

As I walk along the upper floor towards Leighton's office it feels like this is where the grown-ups are based and the kids are downstairs. I really hate working in a bank. Quite a crowd of us headed straight off to careers in the finance sector after A levels, all inspired by the Michael Douglas movie *Wall Street*. Sold on a dream of sharp suits, living in spacious loft conversion flats in central New York, making lots of money, drinking cocktails at flashy bars, driving a Ferrari and meeting glamorous models. Instead, I have a learner motorbike, live in my childhood bedroom, have stayed in the town I grew up in and barely have enough money to last the month. It's safe to say things have not quite gone to plan and Douglas has a lot to answer for. It has not been ideal at home either since Mum died a few years ago. So I'm paying the same rent to Dad as I would for a shared house. I don't begrudge paying it really as I see it's hard for him, although he would find it easier if he didn't drink and smoke so much. He wouldn't even stop drinking when he got a driving ban a few years ago so I don't think he'll stop now.

I knock on Leighton's door. 'Come,' he says, menacingly. As I enter the room, I see Maxine is sitting there on one of two chairs facing his desk. She looks across and gives me a sheepish smile. He gestures for me to sit down in the vacant chair without making eye contact with me. I have no idea what is going on and Maxine's expression offers no clue either. Has she reported me for doing something? I can hardly be accused of coming on to her as sexual harassment. She did buy me that beer of course; maybe she wants her money back? She can't have it – she got me the wrong one anyway.

'Jez. Maxine has been working with me for the last week on a business project and now I am led to understand that you also have a project to complete. Is that correct?' he asks. Now he looks at me over the top of his glasses.

'Ah yes, I was meaning to…' but he cuts me off. Then for what seems an eternity, he lectures me in front of Maxine about my lack of professionalism, leaving my work to the last minute and being a poor reflection on the bank. He's really starting to annoy me. Occasionally he shoots a look at Maxine, who at least has the decency to look embarrassed. It feels like he's playing to an audience and is thriving on it. It hadn't occurred to me that Maxine would have been in the same situation needing a project, but of course it was obvious on reflection she would. But I'm annoyed she told him about me.

Eventually Leighton stops lecturing me, probably just to catch his breath. After our last encounter I can take it a bit better and am feeling more robust. I even manage to look at the artery increasingly protruding and pulsing in his neck as he spits venom at me. I wonder what it would be like to pop a pencil straight into it and watch it burst like crimson rain all over his office. I might enjoy that.

'So, Jeremy. Are you going to take this assignment seriously if I support you?' he asks me eventually as he relaxes and the pulsing of his blood vessel diminishes. I notice him look over to Maxine to see if he has impressed his audience. She's still staring down at papers on his desk.

I can't now tear my gaze away from the artery in his neck. 'Jeremy, are you listening to me?' he says more loudly and I see it come back to life again, dancing on his neck. I have to shake myself out of its snake charming-like trance.

'Yes Leighton. I'm sorry for leaving this project so late,' I say apologetically. He looks delighted with this.

'Good, Jeremy, good,' he says, licking his lips.

'Although, I do think I still have plenty of time to finish the assignment,' I say, not being able to resist the urge to at least defend myself. 'I would just say that I successfully completed all assignments for my A levels where I gained three B grades, which is not so bad.' I can see from the change in colour of his face that he doesn't much like this answer and my attention is immediately drawn back to the vessel in his neck which is now breakdancing. Another one has now popped up on his temple too, dancing to the same rhythm.

'Why you…' he says, unable to put together a sentence while his breathing has become laboured. Is this what a heart attack looks like? Maxine gives my foot a clip from where she's sitting and as I look at her, I see she's shaking her head.

'Don't!' I can see her mouth silently to me.

It takes a while before Leighton regains his composure and excuses us both from his office. I could recognise he did have a point that I have indeed left the assignment late and his time is much more valuable than mine. A point he was keen to make repetitively, beating his stubby finger on the desk. Oh how I would have loved to have stapled it there.

'You shouldn't have answered back like that,' says Maxine after we close Leighton's office door behind us. A couple of the senior clerks look up at us from their desks. They must have heard the ruckus in their boss's office, he was not quiet. I just grunt and walk fast to outpace her – I really don't want to speak right now.

Maxine tries to keep up as we approach the stairs. 'Jez, I'm sorry I told him about you,' she says, 'but I was trying to help and he asked if anyone else was doing the same project. I didn't know what to do.' I forgo my coffee break and make my way back to the counter so I don't have to speak with her. What a drag; I'll now need to work with her on the connected projects Leighton has given us.

Over the next few weeks, we work together in our lunch breaks and some evenings, all supplemented by a further couple of calmer meetings with Leighton to discuss our progress. Maxine is really not too bright; not entirely stupid, but mostly devoid of creativity and original thought, so that has to come from me. Eventually our work is done and I think quite reasonably so. We both have to explain our findings to Leighton who seems vaguely pleased with our understanding of trial balances, and of how to assess the loaning requirement for two very different businesses in our connected scenarios. It's all so dull. Of course, he has more praise for Maxine than for me, but I don't mind even though it's clearly misplaced. His assessment is not shared by the business course tutors who give me an A grade and Maxine a C. Her work was solid enough; I'd checked out the calculations for her, but her analysis did lack that extra spark. I don't think she could have done so well in her A levels and I guess that showed. Class will out.

'Well done,' she says to me in the pub on the night we pick up our grades. Some of the other college crowd are looking glum over their beers. I can see Vicky and Clara sitting down at a table. It looks like Vicky's crying. Presumably she didn't do well. Maxine catches me looking over at them as we stand with our drinks. I have a real ale this time, not lager, and I hope she notices this for future reference.

'I would leave them to it,' she says.

'You think?' I say. 'They shouldn't take it so seriously, it's just an assignment.'

'No. I hear Simon has broken up with Vicky,' says Maxine.

'Oh really?' I say, taking a bit more interest now in what she says. This could be an opportunity to ask Vicky out, but maybe not tonight, tears are a bit of a mood killer. Maybe later if she stops crying – I wonder if she is a sex on the first date kind of girl?

'Yes, apparently he caught an STD from a toilet seat and his mum made him fly home to get it treated.' I suppress a laugh.

'A toilet seat?' I ask.

'Yes, apparently it's very common but now he says he wants to go back overseas "to find himself" as soon as it's treated. He's told her it's all over, too. She's heartbroken.'

'So he's still in the UK now?' I ask. Maxine nods.

'Until he gets it fixed up anyway I think,' she says.

'But he's going back and they're definitely finished?' I ask.

'Seems so. What a bastard,' she says. The night has just gotten a lot better and my mood becomes even brighter. On reflection it could be better to wait a few weeks before making a move on Vicky – that would at least mean I was sure she was clear of STDs too. I did think it might take the whole year for their relationship to implode, but it's amazing it was just a matter of weeks. Simon always was a bit of an idiot. He must have gone crazy with those prostitutes.

I've always been very careful over wearing protection with girls, although I'm admittedly not so experienced. A few clumsy fumbles here and there supplemented by some occasional, drunken one-night stands with some of the easier girls from school. Vicky would be a step up in class and that's quite exciting.

The junior bankers from my course are feeling like making a night of it. There are five guys and six girls I vaguely know from neighbouring banks and I guess we have some sort of a bond. The males are all average looking so I would certainly be the pick of the crowd, even with my matted motorbike hair. So we all finish our drinks and I agree to go on to the bright lights of Abingdon's only nightclub. As we walk out of the pub, Maxine is annoyingly sticking to my side and I worry people will assume we are a couple. I would much rather get closer to the smaller cluster behind us which includes Vicky and Clara.

'Just wait a minute,' says Maxine as we walk along the roadside. She pulls out her purse as we approach a cash machine. 'I need to get some money.'

'OK, no problem,' I say, although irritated I can't shake her off.

I look behind to see where the others are and thankfully they're closing in to join us. Vicky seems less upset now. I wonder if tonight really is too soon for me to make a move on her, or even how she might respond. But if I don't make a move then I could miss out entirely, and she is pretty hot. I could happily be the rebound guy for her – I wouldn't mind that. I don't object to being used if it helps her recovery. Maxine rejoins the main group but now she's looking upset.

'What's up?' I ask as she uses her shoulders to bustle in between Clara and one of the other guys to stroll beside me.

'I'm overdrawn,' she whispers in my ear.

'Oh,' I say. We both know what this means tomorrow when we are back at work. 'Good luck with Leighton.'

The Present Tale

I worked at Francis Drake University for four years, which was quite long enough. Quite why a university in Cumbria should name itself after a slave-trading, warmongering pirate from Plymouth is beyond me and as far as I can tell, everyone else too. I'll have to ask someone one day. I rarely stay anywhere for too long, but I enjoyed it there until a better post came up at USL. Why did I move? Sure they gave me a chair of business management position but I was also made pro-vice-chancellor. It was fundamentally a better position at USL than at Drake's and a better university too. But if you're a leader in higher education, you will know the mantra of a senior manager – stay just long enough so whatever new initiatives you put in place can look good, but not so long that they can go wrong. Which of course they almost always do, so working in cycles of three to four years is best in my experience. Go in, dazzle a bit with some exciting new ideas and then move on before anyone notices you screwed it up. You then blame the next guy, except if he has any sense, he will do the same and blame his predecessor and so it continues. This is the very essence of senior university management – blame it on someone else. I reached the end of my Drake's cycle without signs of obvious screw up, although of course I knew they were there.

My career plan is to become a vice-chancellor just

like Don, but preferably without being murdered. Vice-chancellor is the pinnacle position of a university, the ultimate power, and that is what I want. I will obviously do whatever I need to get there, too. Absolutely whatever it takes. My role as pro-vice-chancellor at USL places me only two steps away from vice-chancellor – deputy vice-chancellor (DVC) next and then the top job. The tricky stage is getting a DVC post. Our DVC at USL, David Lees, is probably two or three years from retirement so that could work out. But for now, my role at USL is pretty reasonable. It's only a couple of hours away from home, I can travel there and back in a day, but it's also far enough away that I need to have a midweek flat to be nearer to the office. This leaves me free to privately indulge my more nefarious habits yet be close enough to home that I can be there when I want.

One day I think I might come back to work at Drake's. It's certainly the kind of place that could give me a start as vice-chancellor as it did for Don. By moving away to USL, it also makes me a more attractive candidate too. In academia, the logic seems to be that if someone else thinks I am OK to appoint into a senior role then I must be alright. Internal promotions always seem so much more difficult to land – if you do a good job, they just want you to keep on doing it. It's a screwed-up philosophy really.

Drake's is a university devoid of self-confidence, almost exclusively catering for a handful of local students. However, the board would never appoint someone from within the organisation to become its leader. Don was an external appointment, a happy idiot you might say. He was lucky too – it was his good fortune to be the grandson to the first vice-chancellor, the Reverend Chaucer, and he claimed he was related all the way back to Geoffrey Chaucer of *The Canterbury Tales* fame. He was less lucky to unwittingly sexually pester the mistress of a serial killer. In that sense, Don was both my victim and inspiration. If Don could be a vice-chancellor, so could I. He should be pleased really; he demonstrated that someone of limited ability and questionable dress sense could get to the top in higher education. What an example for an aspiring academic leader. Anything is therefore possible in this game and he is the very epitome of social mobility. So, the idea of being a vice-chancellor is appealing and if I am nothing else, I'm certainly more stylish than Don.

★★★

It's been almost an hour since the janitor tried her key in the door. Some anxiety is creeping in and I wonder whether I should have run after her to properly control the situation. I don't want to go to prison. It's a common stereotype I know, but I really am too pretty for that. Even though I'm now in my forties I still look quite fine and ladies of a particular age seem drawn to me. A flick of the hair here or there, being excessively agreeable and tactile are all dead giveaways of sexual interest and most women I meet over thirty-five do this in our conversations. My advantage over most men is that I show no sign yet of going bald or even have greying hair. I also work out regularly, have stayed highly sexed and I'm generally much more comfortable in the company of women. Although nowadays it's probably fair to say they also come on to me because of my leadership role. I wonder if this is what Bella was subconsciously doing to Don – did he interpret her friendliness as an invitation? My mind drifts to the thought of his pale white, sweaty body and his crocodile smile. I also imagine Bella unzipping his trousers, which starts to enrage me. I had to kill him before that image could ever have the opportunity to turn into reality. Nevertheless, I'm disappointed the thought hasn't yet left me. I think I can trust her, but then of course her husband probably thinks that too.

I try to control my anxiety about the whereabouts of the janitor with some deep breathing and I begin to relax. Thinking objectively, I don't see how she would have recognised my voice. It was quite a good impression and I have always been told I'm a good mimic. When I was a kid I used to do a decent Elvis impersonation, or at least I thought so.

'Jez, do that impersonation for your dad,' Gran told me one day when I'd been goofing around at her house thinking I was the reincarnation of the King.

'Oh Gran, do I have to?' I said, protesting while at the same time planning which song I should try.

'Go on, Jez, it's terrific,' she said. I made a few more moderate protests as she assembled an audience of herself, my sister Lorraine and Dad. I must have been ten years old and as I stood in front of my austere, hungover father, holding a hairbrush as a microphone in my hand and with my right leg ready to shake like Elvis, I suddenly felt like the ten-year-old I was. I was not Elvis Presley, just a young boy in a tracksuit singing loudly with a pre-pubescent voice and holding a brush. It was like waking from a bad dream and as

I sang 'Hound Dog', I could hear myself with total clarity for the first time. I could see the same realisation written across Dad's grimacing face too, while my gran clapped like a seal and my sister smirked sarcastically. Curse the facilitating nature of over-eager grandparents. So I didn't do it again and instead I've kept all my mimicking to simple social satire of the weak and vulnerable. Nevertheless, my skills are quite good now, so I ought not to worry too much about pretending to be Don. In any case, no security guards or police have yet pounced on me, so I'm probably OK.

It's time to move now. It's 9 p.m. and cautiously I unlock Don's door to poke my head out into the corridor. There's no sign of any janitors, nor any other movement and the ceiling strip lights are all off. If I move around too much the motion sensors will detect me and the lights will spring back on. I'm not really going to be able to help that, but when it happens it could alert security to my presence. However, if they are still operating on the same schedule as when I worked here, then there will be a one-hour window from 9 p.m. where the on-duty guard visits the student dorms at the other end of the campus. So I'll just give it ten minutes and then carry Don down to his car, pop him on the back seat and drive him away. I feel an inner calm at the thought of this achievable plan.

I take a last look around Don's office and all seems well. His DNA will be expected to be here, while as a former employee, my DNA is broadly explainable too. All I need to do is avoid the security cameras and I know those are a rarity here. The resolution of the camera at the exit barrier is only just about good enough to make out the outline of cars and certainly does not have the clarity to see within vehicles. There was the notorious case a few years ago when the cameras weren't even good enough to see the registration number of some thieves' van who ripped the on-campus ATM from the wall. Even then Drake's didn't get a better system. The bank wouldn't let us have another ATM after that as no one would insure it. But as a former member of the leadership team at Drake's, I doubt they would have invested in updating that – Don spent any available money on being 'student centred', even turning the main lecture theatre into a student cinema. Anything to buy their favour.

Thinking of his idiocy annoys me, so I deliver a heavy kick to the ribs of his corpse, but it's interesting to see he doesn't move like a live body anymore, although some air does escape out through his mouth. His eyes are rolled back in his head, so it's safe to assume he is properly dead. But the weight of his body and the lack of any anticipatory recoil as I kicked him has caused me some pain. I curse him for giving me a mild sprain as I rub my ankle. This means rigor mortis is setting in too, which is a drag as he's going to feel really heavy when I carry him to his car. I haven't bothered to wrap him up, so I hope he doesn't ooze too much fluid on the way – that will be a giveaway. Wrapping him up seemed excessive; if you're seen carrying something that looks the shape of a body then no one is realistically going to believe it's anything other than a body. So what's the point? As far as I can see, he isn't seeping out any liquid other than when he urinated as I suffocated him. Even then it was only a moderate trickle down his trouser leg, so perhaps he'd recently been to the loo. I thought he might have fully opened his bowels in his fright, so I was impressed he remained relatively clean. I dabbed the minor spill he made on the carpet with his sweater that had been lying on his sofa. He was not one for expensive clothing that's for sure. You would think a vice-chancellor might make a bit more of a sartorial effort.

I take a deep breath as I lift Don's body and put him over my shoulder. I turn the handle of his office door, being careful not to catch his head on the frame as I walk out. He's really heavy and as I'm fit, he has to be quite a weight, probably 110-120 kilograms. Glancing back at the room I exit through the door, scanning one last time for anything I might have left behind, then check the time on my Omega wrist-watch: it's 9.10 p.m. It all seems OK; no sign of blood, nothing disturbed. Although he had been surprised to see me, Don hadn't struggled, so there was no real mess. He'd just shaken involuntarily for a while when he fell off his chair. Fifty thousand volts from the police Taser I acquired from the Dark Web will do that to you. I'd tested it on the neighbour's golden retriever beforehand, but then a dog is a lot smaller than 110-kilogram Don. It was admittedly a bit of a lazy trial run, but I couldn't easily find a bigger animal to test it on. I suppose I could have gone out to a farm and fired it at a sheep or a cow, but as the neighbours were out and the dog was being noisy in their yard it seemed like a good opportunity. So, I scaled their small back fence and faced up to it like I was a gunslinger in Dodge City. Golden retrievers aren't the most aggressive animals and so it just stopped barking, looked at me quizzically for a moment and panted with its big floppy tongue hanging out of the side of its mouth. I took a jinking step to the side so as to get a good aim at its midriff, as it stood confused, and I fired the Taser into its belly. It really shook as the electrodes hit. I must admit being relieved it hadn't died. It took the retriever almost twenty minutes to regain its composure and he had wet himself, hence I assumed Don might do the same. If the dog had died there may have been some questions so I'm glad it pulled through. Although whenever he sees me now he backs off, whimpers a bit and hides behind his owners. It does perhaps look suspicious when I see him or talk with them, but he doesn't bark. That's electrotherapy for you. Pavlov would be proud of me – operant conditioning of a dog proven in reality, although in a slightly different experimental design than he originally intended.

I carefully close Don's door behind me and I hear it latch. Stepping into the corridor, the florescent lights automatically trigger to spring on, but as predicted there's no sign of any security staff. As I struggle on my way towards the stairs, I glance through the windows to see that the car park appears empty and there are no flashing blue lights anywhere. The fact that no one is working late is a relief but it's also exasperating that people leave so early these days – this is not a proper university. No one here works much after 5 p.m. and they will never get ahead like that. I huff and puff a bit under his weight as I descend one flight of stairs to the ground floor, distracting myself with thoughts of my early days when academics actually cared about their performance and worked long hours. When I started out I was surrounded by workaholics but admittedly most of that time was in Australia where they are all more competitive and it was at a completely different kind of a university. Drake's is for snowflake students, overseen by snowflake staff.

Reaching Don's car, I use his remote fob to unlock it, and with a last effort, I slide his body into the back seats. He is not a tall man, so he fits snugly and doesn't need contorting. I slam the door, put on my white biohazard suit and move around to the driver's side. I feel my heart rate start to decrease – that was quite an effort.

I press the ignition, turn the headlights to the dim lights setting and drive carefully towards the exit barrier. I look side to side out of the corners of my eyes but see no one. The barrier raises as I approach it and I drive straight through. I check my watch for the time – 9.20 p.m. – and my next stop is Discovery Woods to bury him.

The Tale of the Bank

I wake up at home the next morning having not propositioned Vicky in the nightclub. There just was not the right opportunity, and besides, she was revelling in the attention from the other bank guys. One of them, Damian, has a car and they seemed to be getting friendly so I left them to it. It would serve him right if he caught Simon's STD from her. The place was mostly empty and even Maxine wasn't there to chat to – she didn't have the entrance money so I think she caught a bus home.

Dad is up and awake already and giving Lorraine a lift to work. Lorraine is a nightmare; always spiteful and in a bad mood, so I basically stay out of her way. If I am in her way, she gets her much older boyfriend Trevor to poke me in the chest and tell me to back off. He hasn't ever hit me or anything, but I can tell he does weights so he would damage me. If I'm nice to her, he tells me he'll take me to the gym sometime, so that sounds a fair deal.

Dad and Lorraine tend to set off at 8 a.m. so I just lie in until I hear the door slam closed. I give Clara a prod to wake up. Vicky might not have been interested, but Clara had looked bored last night so we hooked up. She was far too drunk to drive herself home, yet OK to ride on the back of my bike, even without a helmet. I could have given her mine, I guess, but she was too drunk to ask and I didn't offer. She was pretty wild, but not so wild as to wake Dad or Lorraine. I'll take her to the bus stop soon so we'll need to get up rapidly now, have showers, and I still have yet to style my hair, although I really don't know why I bother.

It's not a long journey to work, only fifteen minutes or so on the bike. Clara was still drowsy and a bit whiny to easily shake loose this morning, even after I made her a cup of coffee. She was a little upset to face the embarrassment of being in the same clothes for work again today. I expect her colleagues could notice, but I doubt it's the first time she's been in this situation.

'I'll call you,' I say, as I point her in the direction of the bus stop. She nods and smiles at me. I don't think I will though, she's too easy.

I get to work at my usual time of 8.45 a.m., which is just as well, as anyone arriving after 8.50 a.m. gets their name coloured in highlighter pen in the sign-in book. I see the usual bunch of men in ill-fitting suits and women in poorly designed uniform skirts milling around the entrance when I get there. It seems unfair to me that men have to pay for suits and women get to wear free bank clothes; even if those clothes are not in any way stylish. At least they are tight though, so you can see which of the female staff have good figures, and the white blouses they wear are essentially transparent in the right lighting. Some of them have already managed to get themselves a coffee but most just look sleepy, or is it depressed? I'm not sure. I deposit my helmet, gloves, coat and wet-weather trousers in a locker, make myself a cup of instant coffee and head to the counter.

The morning passes uneventfully until 9.30 a.m. when I notice Maxine heading off upstairs, presumably to see

Leighton to talk about her overdrawn account. I imagine she might have been through this drill a few times with him. He seemed to like her in our meetings so I doubt she will get the full treatment I got, but I will be interested to hear how it goes.

Time passes slowly over the morning, but I don't notice Maxine come back down after almost an hour. That's a very long time for a telling-off about being overdrawn. I have a quiet moment without customers at the counter and so take a quick look at my account balance and then also scan down to check out Maxine's too. Ouch, she's £109 in deficit.

I see Maxine come slowly down the stairs just after 10.30 a.m. She looks a bit flushed and when I look over to her, she avoids eye contact. She settles back at her desk and gets on with some paperwork while I continue to watch. I leave her alone after that as she doesn't seem to want to engage. So, for the rest of the day I simply get into my routine. The counter is pretty busy so the day goes fairly quickly. One of the reasons I think I'm on the counter is that I very rarely make any mistakes with money so the till has a very good chance of balancing at the end of the day. My rotation in this role is also longer than anyone else I believe, or so some people say. I think a few of the other juniors are getting a bit jealous of that and want their turn so they can get out of some of the more laborious jobs we are expected to do.

Sometimes the counter does not balance properly at the end of the day and then we all have to stay until it does, or until we can pinpoint the problem. It's not an efficient use of everyone's time to do that and when you get new juniors on the counter everyone groans as they know errors will be made. It's a relief to all when someone experienced is in this role. One time not long after I started, the counter was £1000 short. Everyone looked at me as the most likely culprit, being new. I could see in their eyes the look of suspicion and also annoyance that I was the reason people were kept late. In the end it turned out the chief cashier of the time had given a company £1000 too much when she made up cash wages. Fortunately they were honest enough to report it the next day. It was annoying to feel under suspicion like that when I hadn't done anything. But at least it wasn't my error and after that I seem to have been viewed in a positive light for some reason; they're probably just relieved I'm not a thief.

'Are you OK?' I say to Maxine as we collect our coats at the end of the day.

'Why shouldn't I be?' she sounds snappy, but I only asked. She scuttles away and off to catch her bus home. I wonder if she heard I took Clara home last night? Clara is not a quiet type so it's probably already gossip. I hadn't really expected Clara to come home with me and I think both of us only really got together through boredom. It was a fun evening in the end, but I hope it doesn't affect my chances with Vicky.

I make my way home. Lorraine is there with Trevor. I know he's married so I don't see why he tries to hide it, but she hasn't told Dad this news. That could be interesting to watch as I doubt he would approve. It's the talk of the town too, or at least several people I know have independently mentioned it to me. She just likes the gifts he gives her. She has a whole bunch of new clothes in her wardrobe now, a new TV and an even more condescending attitude than usual.

'Jez – phone!' she shouts as I enter the house, before I can put down my helmet, take off my gloves and restyle my matted hair.

'Hello?' I say, answering the phone.

'Hi. It's me,' says a female voice.

'Clara?' I ask.

'No, it's Maxine,' she says.

'Ah,' I say. She doesn't say anything for a while probably hoping I will explain why I answered by saying 'Clara', but I decide not to – she called me.

'Sorry about earlier,' she says eventually. She sounds flustered.

'It's OK, no problem,' I say. We all have bad days and dealing with Leighton was never going to be a good one for her. I wonder whether she's heard about Clara coming home with me and is going to ask me about that. It's really none of her business. I've never given her any encouragement, although in an emergency at the end of a boozy night I'd probably give in. The phone call is a bit stilted – she wants to say something but won't tell me what it is and I'm really not too good at casual chat.

'I don't have anyone to talk to,' she says and I try not to groan. She might be a nice girl, but she isn't my problem. I guess she thinks we bonded over our project work. I never really asked if she had a boyfriend so I don't want to get too involved now if she's having relationship issues.

'You're such a good listener,' she says, which I assume is a joke so I let out a small laugh. 'You're funny too,' she says. I think she's deluded, but I can hear sniffing in the background and it sounds like stifled tears. I really am not a good listener and was already distracted in this conversation wondering who Liverpool FC were playing at the weekend. Sometimes people positively disposed towards me assume the absence of talking is quiet reflection, but it's not.

'It's OK, Maxine. It'll be OK,' I say. It seems the right thing to say in the circumstances although I have no real idea what will be OK. I hope she doesn't press me about it. I can hear her crying intensifying now so I'm not sure if this was the right tact.

'You are so sweet, Jez. Could you come and meet me?' she says.

'Oh,' I say. I hadn't expected that to be her answer so this was a miscalculation.

'I'm not sure I can get away,' I say, scrambling to think of an excuse. But she's crying harder now. I imagine this is what being in a relationship must be like. Or a sexless relationship anyway. I don't have plans for the evening and in the absence of an adequate reason not to go, I end up agreeing and so grab my coat.

I meet Maxine in the Black Prince pub in Abingdon. It is not the greatest pub, but then Abingdon is not the best town. It is such a sleepy place – full of retirees and neglected businesses. Maxine is there already waiting for me. She must have found some access to cash as she already has a drink, but she doesn't seem to have gotten me one this time. I wave at her, but she has already seen me and smiles in my direction. I go to the bar to order myself a beer – at least I only have to buy myself one now. I take a sip of the beer on my way over to her table. They do have good local beer here; Morlands is the local brewery but the regional newspaper is always running stories that they are on the point of closure. This is a situation not helped much by our bank as Morlands have their business with us. They've probably had vein-pulsing conversations with Leighton, too.

'Hi,' she says as I sit down. At least she's not crying now. She looks pleased to see me.

'So, what's up?' I say. I really hope it's not boyfriend trouble; I could do without spending the evening talking about problems with other guys. She doesn't speak for a while and keeps rubbing the rim of her glass and I wonder if she is trying to make it squeak, but she would need to rub it faster for that. We sit like this for a while and I begin to wonder why I'm here.

'It's Leighton. You must promise not to tell anyone,' she says forcibly, staring at me and reaching across the table to hold my hand.

'OK,' I say.

An hour later as I drive through the dark lanes back home I come to two conclusions. Firstly, I really do dislike banking and think I should do something else for a career. Secondly, Leighton really is a bastard to take advantage of Maxine. I can feel a cold shiver of excitement develop in the base of my spine as I think of what I would like to do to him.

The Tale of an Awakening

Autumn, 1991

Turning twenty is no big deal. It's evidently also not a big deal for my family who have either forgotten or chosen to ignore it. Mum was always the one to observe milestones but now she's gone, celebrations have mostly disappeared off the schedule.

'You're having a party on Saturday, Jez and that's that,' Maxine said to me at work on Friday. Since when did she take over running my life? I cringed as she said it and even more so when she then invited everyone else in the office.

'I'll be there for sure,' says Dennis from mortgages. Dennis smells. I can't quite place it, but it's urine-infused and deeply unpleasant.

'Oh great,' I say, trying not to breathe through my nostrils. I'm not sure if anyone has ever told him, perhaps I should?

'There you go, people are keen to come,' says Maxine afterwards as Dennis moves on, thankfully taking his odour with him. She looks pleased with herself. Although I don't think we should use Dennis as the benchmark of an acceptable level of attendance. I doubt he gets out much.

'But I don't want a party,' I say. I'm not even sure how she knows it's my birthday tomorrow. I suspect she might have looked up my personnel file – maybe I should complain to human resources about it.

'You're having a party and I'm going to organise it!' she says, forcefully.

'But… ' I say. I don't get the chance to finish before she's gone.

'Just go with it, mate,' says Brian from personal loans, patting me on the back. Brian is a toucher, one of those tactile people who use every opportunity to get their hands on you, whether you are male or female. I don't think he's gay, or at least I'm not sure, but he is the office hugger. If someone is upset, you don't have to wait long for Brian to turn up like a magnet, hug at the ready. At least Dennis is not a hugger.

'She isn't even my girlfriend,' I say, but Brian isn't listening.

***

So it's Saturday evening and I'm in a pub in Oxford with an indiscriminate bunch of bankers for my birthday who couldn't care less about me and who all look completely uncomfortable in each other's company. As I sip my beer, I look among the crowd and realise I wouldn't recognise most of them outside of the bank. To some extent wearing a suit is a great leveller, a bit like a school uniform guaranteeing a general standard of elegant presentation. That is apart, of course, from the more sartorially aware like me who can tell the difference in levelness. I saved for months to be able to buy the two suits I alternate for work wear. Neither of them are tailor-made, I can't afford that, but they are nicely cut and they fit me well. I doubt anyone else there notices my navy-blue suit is Hugo Boss and the grey one is Calvin Klein, no one has ever said anything. But I know the difference between a designer suit and a mass-produced one bought at a retail outlet, so that's the main thing.

'Another drink, Jez?' asks Dennis. He still smells, even on a night out, although his clothes look clean. It could be because he's a generally sweaty type, which I think is always a problem when you are that fat.

'No, you're OK, I've still got most of this pint,' I say. His glass is empty and so he waddles off to the bar to get himself another.

'Enjoying yourself?' asks Maxine, rocking gently to the music from the jukebox as she closes in on me. It's a track by Erasure, I'm not sure which one as they're a bit samey. It's catchy though, so I hum along, nodding my head in time to the music. How cool I must look.

'Yes, great,' I say, taking a sip of my beer as she stands next to me. I take a look around the crowd but can't see any sign of Clara or Vicky.

'I'm glad,' says Maxine and she gently rubs my shoulder, which creeps me out a bit.

'Did you invite anyone from the other branches of the bank?' I ask.

'You mean Clara?' she asks.

'Well her, Vicky and the others,' I say.

'No,' she says and stops rubbing my shoulder.

The night plods on, I have a few more beers but not as many as Brian who has taken hugging to a new level by 11 p.m. I see across the room that Maxine looks upset about something and Brian is comforting her. Any second and he will have her in a bear hug. The group is breaking up somewhat now and I'm thinking of quietly making a run for it. The next bus will be soon and I could make it. I'm not sure anyone would notice now. I look around for the closest exit and can't see any of our crowd between me and the door. Taking a final sip of my beer, I place the empty glass on the nearest table, excuse myself from a conversation I haven't been following with two plain girls from personal banking and take my leave. I notice Brian is now embracing Maxine and if I'm not mistaken he has his hand on her backside. So I guess he isn't gay after all.

Leaving the pub I'm staggering a little, but generally sound. I need to head towards the bus stop as a night of heavy drinking is not one for the motorbike. At this time, the buses only run hourly and so as I take a glance at my latest Casio digital watch, I see I have ten minutes to catch it. It's approximately twelve minutes to the bus stop from here so I take a short cut through a college alleyway between Carfax and the Abingdon Road where my bus will soon depart. This will shave off the necessary one or two minutes without the need for me to run, which will save me sweating into the fabric of my Lacoste shirt.

'Do you have any change?' I am startled as someone asks me from out of the darkness. A figure comes out of the shadows. I can't see his face properly, but he looks around my age, skinny and wearing a hoodie. His hood is up, but it is not so cold as to warrant it.

I'm in a rush for the bus and so I make a gesture to pat myself down as if to say I have no money, which is usually the case. But unhandily I hear a 'chink' in my pocket, forgetting I have retained some necessary coins for the bus fare.

'No, sorry I don't,' I say, as the coins jangle noisily telling him otherwise.

'Are you taking the piss?' comes the voice again and this time I can see his shape more clearly as he catches the streetlight from the main road at the far end of the alley. I see now he is in his mid-twenties, unshaven, and has a few pockmarks. Above his left eyebrow he has a small homemade tattoo, but I can't make out what it's supposed to be. It looks a mess – the kind of casual indifference to making such a major cosmetic decision that means he would never get a job in a bank. He is indeed skinny and his hoodie has several stains on it of differing shapes and sizes. He walks towards me and looks angry. As he gets closer, I think of Dennis and wonder if I had overreacted to his personal odour as this is on a completely different scale. He's right on me now and I can even smell his breath, which I can only really describe as eggy.

'Look, I'm sorry, but I'm in a hurry to catch my bus,' I say. I try to move to the side of him, but he moves with me, staying in the way.

'Do you think you're better than me, is that it?' he says.

'No, but I do have to catch my bus.'

He's standing directly in front of me now and pushes me backwards with the flat of his right hand. My first thought is to look down at my shirt as his grubby hand is sure to have left a stain. God knows where it has been.

'You're not going anywhere. Take the piss out of me by shaking your change would you?'

'Look, I don't want any trouble.'

'You toffs are all the same.'

I'm no toff, but admittedly my elocution is a lot better than his, he sounds very regional. I quickly try to reassure him of my working-class origins but he's having none of it.

'Just let me pass,' I say eventually. But as I look in his eyes I see hate there and realise I could be in some trouble.

'Give me all your money, you posh prat,' he says as he steps back to retrieve a knife from the front pouch of his hoodie. It feels strange to be faced by someone holding a weapon. It's very unusual and not wholly unexciting.

I can't say specifically what next comes over me. I don't feel scared, or angry so much as turned on and I grab the knife from his hand at such speed that I can see the rage in his eyes instantly replaced by fear.

'Look just forget… ' he says, now trying to back away from me. But I don't let him and as I hold him with my left hand around his dirty neck, I plunge his knife into his belly. I feel it breaking through his flesh, hear him gasp and watch his eyes become big and startled. How exciting this is, so I gasp too as we share an intimate look, almost sexual, then breathing in the moment as if I am newly born. I'm not sure what happened in the next thirty seconds or so. All I know is when I draw my next conscious breath, I look down to see the knife in my right hand and it's now completely covered in blood. It's all his blood and he's lying on the ground at my feet. He's not moving and I give him a little kick to see if there's a response but he doesn't move or make a sound. It seems wrong somehow not to know his name and I feel a desire to know him and for him to know me and that I have been the one responsible to end his life. We are bonded now and should know one another. I decide to give him a name – Daniel. I shall honour him with this name so I will always remember him, Daniel and his eggy breath. I look at my shirt and see it's in an appalling state, completely crimson with Daniel's blood.

I stand there for a minute just looking at him, tilting my head slightly to look from different angles, absorbing the moment and committing it to memory. I need to remember this moment for ever and, for some reason, I start to hum along to the Erasure track I heard earlier, now remembering it's 'A Little Respect' and I feel myself dancing along to it on the spot as I look at his wounds. This is so exciting; the song title sounds so apt and I will remember it, this moment, and Daniel for ever.

Daniel's wounds look painful, not that he can feel them anymore – I must have gotten quite carried away. I stop dancing and crouch over him to get a closer look. I can't see any sign of life, but I don't want to touch him – he looks pretty dead. I can see there must be at least five puncture wounds to his chest and a deep one to his neck. I don't recollect doing that one at all – how weird. On the ground next to him, I notice part of a finger and know it isn't mine. I think I might have sliced one off at some point, probably as he tried to protect himself. A court could take a dim view of that kind of thing, perhaps perversely even seeing him as the victim and his wounds as defensive. That would not be ideal.

The Tale of an Awakening

As I compose myself standing over Daniel, I begin to appreciate the precariousness of my situation. I retreat into the shadow of the alley, away from the streetlight for a moment but still gripping Daniel's knife in my hand. I look around and thankfully see no one else, but there could be at any time. I hear a noise and for a moment I feel I'm being watched. I sense the presence of another, but as I scan the area, I see no one. There must be people close by and unless I want to be discovered, I will need to move quickly. I keep the knife and make my way towards the main road. Poking my head out of the alley I see a bicycle rack by the entrance to one of the colleges and so I make my way towards it stealthily trying to stay out of sight. The knife is handy and I use it to cut through one of the easier cord-based fastenings to free up a reasonable-looking mountain bike. Placing the knife in my sock I pedal away rapidly, mentally working out a route that will mean I can avoid main roads on my way home. But it's a long way to cycle home from Oxford.

Along my route I stop a couple of times to avoid vehicles, and on the second occasion to dispose of the knife into the River Thames. I wonder how many weapons and secrets that river holds. I feel proud to have contributed to that story, mine and Daniel's story. Daniel and his eggy breath. As I cycle away from the river I see a row of shabby council houses and one of them has a variety of children's toys strewn over their front lawn. I also see they've left their washing on the line and so I stop to pick through their appalling, cheap high street clothes. However, I do find a large, heavy sweater that although still a bit damp is adequate to cover up my own blood-stained shirt. It's not a cold evening so this extra layer will make me sweat, but it could normalise my appearance to any casual observers.

I'm not much of a cyclist and so the eight-mile trip from Oxford is hard work with a couple of tricky hills. You would think they would be easy enough on a mountain bike, but I'm having trouble with the gears. Eventually I start to recognise my surroundings and when I'm a mile from home, I discard the bicycle in my old high school cycle rack. Someone is sure to steal it from there. It was a terrible school.

My walk on the final mile home is uneventful and it's good to be off the bike now. I haven't looked in the mirror, but I can tell from the taste of the sweat running from my forehead into my mouth that there must be some of Daniel's blood on my face. This could be quickly apparent if I were closely inspected or stopped by the police. So I skip from shadow to shadow trying to avoid street lights. A couple of streets from home I discard the sweater in a convenient bin and finally, I creep back into our house by the back door.

Checking the time on the kitchen clock I see it's 2 a.m. All's quiet so I decide to completely strip down and place all my clothes in the washing machine, being sure to add some stain remover. I set the machine to ten degrees hotter than is sensible and cross my fingers that this will be adequate to remove all remnants of blood. It's annoying that it's well above the suggested temperature for my Lacoste shirt, but I think I might need to sacrifice it on this occasion.

As I hear the washing machine fill with water and start to spin, I decide to take a shower, instantly feeling the relief of hot clean water running over my body. I look down at the cubicle floor as I wash my hair and see the water is slightly pink. There are a few clumps of what looks like coagulated blood amid the soapy foam as it runs off my body. I must have looked pretty bad while cycling. I start to relax and think about how I want to spend the weekend ahead. Neither Vicky nor Clara was there for my birthday but I wonder if they might be available to go out if I called? Clara has been trying to hook up again, but I have put her off thus far. Maybe I should reconsider her – I expect sleeping with her has blown it for me with Vicky anyway. I look down at the cubicle floor before turning off the water and I see nothing but clean water now.

The Tale of an Awakening

Over the weekend I look for news about Daniel in the national and local newspapers, but I see no sign of anything. I'd feel more comforted to hear he was at least confirmed as dead. It could go very badly for me if he isn't; surely he couldn't still be alive?

It isn't until lunchtime on Monday when I pick up a local paper in the bank's staff common room that I'm relieved see a report on Daniel. I recognise his face instantly although he looks a few years younger and cleaner in the photograph. I'm disappointed to see his name is actually Keith. Daniel suited him much better. I decide to stick with Daniel, so I excitedly make myself a coffee and settle down in one of the comfy sofas to read about it in the *Herald*. HORROR SLAYING OF THE HOMELESS it says. It's typical of the local paper to be so dramatic.

'Vicious and sustained attack,' it says, which is also a bit harsh, I feel, as he did initiate the situation. It was an act of self-defence although admittedly I did lose myself in the moment. I think if a court heard the full details, they would recognise I mostly acted quite reasonably, but to stay there at the scene would have been a risk and it's difficult to see how I would get another job in the business sector with this hanging over me. So I did the right thing making my escape. It feels quite an achievement to have pulled it off and I wonder how many other people could say they have done such a thing and gotten away with it? I close my eyes for a moment, humming along quietly to Erasure, and vividly picturing Daniel lying lifeless on the floor. It feels good to have this memory locked away in my private vault, my secret, my adventure, and now it's a flashbulb memory ready to be recalled whenever I want, or whenever I hear that song. As I finish the last of my coffee, I get a warm feeling about it and I glance over to Leighton on the other side of the room. I feel like winking at him, to say, 'You're next,' but restrain the urge. He's delivering a lecture to a couple of his minions as he demolishes a sandwich. I think it's egg and cress but I can't be sure.

The Tale of an Awakening

End

Over the next couple of weeks, I fail to find any further news about Daniel and I'm careful not to bring it up with anyone in conversation at the bank. The police never come to our door either and as time passes, it's not so much relief I feel but disappointment that the excitement is subsiding. It's quite deflating and I am not sure why, as I definitely do not wish to be discovered and end up in prison. So I decide to use this event as motivation to turn my life around and consider the life choices I have made.

The first thing I do is to relentlessly pester Trevor to take me to the gym whenever he comes to visit Lorraine and, eventually, he gives in. This proves very useful as he shows me all the basic free-weight lifting techniques I need in order to properly use weights. After a couple of sessions, I'm confident enough to go on my own and after six weeks or so I can even feel my chest and biceps growing beyond the capacity of my tight-fit T-shirts. This is annoying as they were expensive, but also good as the benefits of a weight-training regime quickly manifest themselves when I start to attract more female attention in nightclubs for my athletic shape. I look so good I decide to accessorise with a spray tan and buy myself a new Hugo Boss plain black T-shirt to wear with my Levi 501s. Not that it helps me with Vicky – she's a lost cause now, particularly after I called Clara up for sex again. Girls don't like you sleeping with their friends apparently. Anyway, she has paired up with a corporate loans guy from her branch now and he's older with his own flat and a car.

The next major thing I need to fix is my career. I've decided I don't fit in the world of banking and my dislike for Leighton is getting overpowering. I've started to fantasise about plunging a knife into his belly as I'd done to Daniel. So I decide to take myself out of the situation for fear of getting overexcited and ending up in prison. I do something I should have done a long time ago after completing my A levels and go to university. I've left it late in the year to do this, but fortunately there are still some places available in the summer clearing process to gain access to the lower-ranked universities. But I don't mind so much; it'll be nice to leave home, go somewhere new and start a different adventure. After a lengthy conversation on the phone with an admissions tutor, I'm offered a place on a Business Administration degree at Sheffield Hallam University. This suits me well as it means I can make a fresh start away from Leighton, my dysfunctional family and also Maxine who is now becoming an irritating constant presence, apparently even telling people she's my girlfriend.

I have to give one week's notice at work and so I quietly plan my exit by securing a student grant from the local council and I pay a deposit for a place in the university halls accommodation. When it's all set up, I let my family and the bank know on the same day. The bank didn't seem at all bothered to lose a junior clerk. Dad is more concerned, which I thought was nice of him, but it transpires he was mostly worried about the loss of rental income. Maxine looked the most upset when Dennis unhelpfully blurted it out in the office. I was hoping I might be able to just quietly slip away. She took a half day's leave to recover from the shock – everyone is now convinced she's my girlfriend.

***

I barely thought about Daniel and his eggy breath while I studied in Sheffield. I was too busy, and for the first time in my life I became really focused on something. I was genuinely interested in academic study, the subjects and the success I was achieving. I had an affinity for the style of learning required in university and it surprised me that I quickly rose near to the top of the class, hindered only from the top spot by Tommy from Chester. But after his untimely death I was more motivated than ever to get ahead and so I really kicked on from there. I put all my skills to good use too, eventually going on to work in London as a trader at an international investment bank. Over the next five years I completed a Master of Business Administration (MBA) degree in the evenings and such was my thirst for study it was quickly followed by a part-time PhD at Brunel University. When I finished my PhD I was told it was a considerable achievement to gain it in such short time. I also became financially comfortable over this time through some shrewd investments using my annual bonuses and some well-hidden knowledge of insider trading.

After being so motivated by my study, I felt strong post-PhD blues and I didn't like it at all. I loved to study and the academic community intrigued me, so I looked for opportunities to become a lecturer in Business. After taking a few guest lectures as an 'industry expert' from the world of investment banking, a position came up in the Business School of Staffordshire University. So, I began my life as an academic and it made me happy and fulfilled. Almost.

The Tale of the Bank

2001

I put the binoculars down on the passenger seat next to me in the blue Nissan Micra I acquired this morning. It smells of dog and old people but I shouldn't complain – it's fit for purpose. The owner had no business driving at her age anyway and as I'd watched her potter up the driveway into her house, I estimated she must have been at least eighty. Her dog was barely a dog at all; one of those small ornament animals you expect to be wearing ribbons and getting a monthly pedicure. It could certainly bark though and it took a couple of stiff kicks to quieten it down.

My prey is in his house and I now just need to wait. I reflect that I have come a long way in the last ten years since I first crossed paths with Daniel and his eggy breath in Oxford. That was when I was a fledgling killer, like a kitten not quite understanding my art, playing at it and without yet having perfected my skills. I'm still not perfect, but I am now an experienced apex predator, ready and excited about my morning of fun.

Despite what you might think, killing is not easy, or rather it's not easy to get away with it. I'm a big ideas kind of guy and my chief concern is that small details bore me. So I worry sometimes that my lack of attention to detail could be my undoing and a few times in recent years I've been rather lucky to get away with things that could have turned ugly. It's the fear of discovery that means I rarely kill and even when I do, it's only after considerable, rather dull planning and when I feel the probability of success is high.

Today's adventure has been a long time coming and the day has benefited from considerable preparatory work. Maxine and I will soon be moving to Australia for me to take up my new academic post as Head of the Business School at Janszoon University in North Queensland, and today represents an opportunity for closure in the last weeks before we leave the UK.

I've always wanted to live somewhere more adventurous, although I'm not averse to returning home at some point. Tropical Queensland is an exciting place, packed full of natural predators. It's a move of significant professional recognition too, showing that I'm really starting to make it in academia. After the PhD, working in the city and then taking some early academic posts, I can now look forward to enjoying the rest of my career in universities, which as far as I can tell are packed full of sociopaths, psychopaths and narcissists just like me.

Maxine is of course ecstatic now we're married. She followed me to Sheffield soon after I started my undergraduate degree and thereafter continued to pester me into submission. She was always around and I suppose if I was uncharitable, I would call her a stalker. None of my undergraduate contemporaries could boast of having their very own stalker and so I was unique. It was funny at first but became irritating when I needed private time or when I found out she'd warned various girls off me. I wondered why my strike rate had dipped and although I told her to back off, she didn't listen. I became her obsession and then one night she surprised me when I was practising my skills on Tommy, my cocky classmate from the business school. I thought no one was around but there she was, watching me at distance as I beat Tommy to death with a dustbin lid behind a service station. But she didn't recoil in horror nor report me to the police – her price for silence was marriage. Why didn't I just kill her? Ask yourself this – why wouldn't a psychopath like the company of someone dedicated to their every whim. We shared the same objectives – mine. So, we got married. It wasn't a big deal; her parents came and cried a lot. My dad came and drank a lot. But getting married seemed to relax her, she gave me a bit more space and didn't ask any more questions of me about Tommy. As far as she knows that was a one-off and she was happy to put it behind us. It worked out well too, as with Tommy out of the way I became the standout graduate of the year so everything started to fall into place nicely. But right now, I have a loose end to tie up before we leave for our new life in Australia. Lying next to the binoculars is my kill kit and I'm twitching with excitement that today is the day I will finally take care of Leighton.

The Present Tale

By the time I get home from burying Don in Discovery Woods, I'm exhausted, dirty, sweaty and in need of sleep. But before I do that, the first thing I need is a shower to free myself of his stench and to cleanse my body. By the time I dropped him into the ground in his new woodland home he had just started to smell, too, the stench of warm meat, brought on by the unseasonably fine weather.

The refreshing sensation of clean, cool water in the shower is very welcome. I inhale the fragrance of my favourite lime shower gel which helps me lose the scent of death from my nostrils. Eventually I feel somewhat refreshed and I pop my head into Maxine's bedroom, quietly taking some fresh Armani pyjamas from the dresser drawer, being careful not to wake her. It proves difficult though as she is a light sleeper and I hear her stir.

'Oh you are so late!' she says dozily as I quietly try to back out of the room. She raises her head slightly from the position she'd been sleeping in, giving out a yawn.

'Yes,' I say. 'Go back to sleep and we can catch up in the morning.'

'Bad traffic?' she asks, ignoring my advice to stay sleeping.

'Yeah. Go to sleep – all fine.' She nods back at me and then rolls over, taking a handful of duvet with her as she settles back down.

I stagger towards the guest room – I now mostly sleep

here; Maxine doesn't like it of course, so I keep my clothes in the main bedroom. But my sleeping pattern is horrendous nowadays and so being in bed with someone else is just torture for me when I'm restless. Seeing the freshly made bed in front of me with its crisp sheets makes me want to collapse straight on to it. I make only a partial effort to undress, putting on my pyjama bottoms and pulling the duvet over me. I rest my head on the pillow and fall asleep almost instantly before I can even reflect happily on a long but successful day.

***

I feel drowsy in the morning but wake anyway when I sense the sunlight creeping into the room. I can see the light between the gaps in the curtains and so I sleepily grapple for my phone on the side table. As I blink and rub my eyes into focus, I can see it's just after 8 a.m. I stretch my arms wide and deeply yawn. I feel much better for having slept, although my arms and neck are really aching as I try to gently rotate my head. Although I regularly exercise in the gym, the motion of carrying a dead body and burying it in the woods is work my muscles are not accustomed to.

Outside the bedroom door I can hear some whispering.

'Why can't I go in there?' I can hear it's Jamie talking and he sounds frustrated.

'You know why. He's had a long journey and needs some sleep,' says Maxine.

'Come on Mum, I haven't seen him all week.' I hear him stamp his foot. I decide to settle back down under the covers to see if I can shake off my drowsiness.

'No, wait until he gets up. He needs to rest,' she says. I hear him sigh and then footsteps going down the stairs – he's given up for now. I think about calling out to him, that it's alright to come in to see me, that I've missed him as much as he's missed me, but I don't. I could use more sleep and so I snuggle back down and try to catch another thirty minutes or so. It works and I drift off again.

When I next wake it's close to 9 a.m. and this time I do feel a lot better although I can still feel my muscles aching, thanks to that damn Don Chaucer. I check my phone to see if I have any messages but there's nothing from Bella. I wonder where she is and what she's doing; my mind drifts to thoughts of her having sex with her husband, although she says she doesn't. But at least it's not an image of her with Don any longer.

Bella tells me she only wants me and not her husband, but I'm not sure I fully believe her. She's far too hot for her husband not to want her sexually, so that just doesn't seem plausible. I'm not sure why I find her so attractive really, it's like she's a drug – something about that dark sun-kissed look southern Europeans have, as if they've grown up on a vineyard, sipping on a crisp white wine and eating olives. I hadn't even noticed her at work until one day I saw her stretch for a periodical on a high shelf in the library. I caught a glimpse of her lace bra between the strain of the buttons on her blouse. As I looked her up and down, I noticed the muscles in her calves as she struggled to reach the book. She obviously worked out. Rather than help her, I took a step back to have a better look. I couldn't quite believe I hadn't noticed her before and from then on, she'd intrigued me.

'Are you OK?' she said when she had retrieved the dusty journal she'd been looking for.

'Yes, sorry, just a bit distracted,' I said, blushing, which was rare for me, but she'd evidently caught me sizing her up.

'I noticed,' she laughed. 'You could have been chivalrous and got it down for me.'

'Yes, I could have, but I didn't want to,' I said, despite my blushes. She looked surprised.

'Well that's not very nice. I think perhaps you are not a very nice man,' she said, laughing.

'No, I'm not a nice man,' I said, which was indeed true but perhaps not in the way she understood it. I smiled provocatively at her, sustaining eye contact longer than was necessary, and she flicked her hair. From that moment, we viewed each other a little differently than we had done previously, exchanging knowing looks in meetings, and within a month we were having sex. That was a few years ago now.

I send a quick message to Bella to say hi, but there's no response. I give her five minutes to answer, but I can see she hasn't read the message. I decide to give up for now and concentrate on something else, so I read the news on my tablet instead.

The main headlines are dominated by talk of the UK leaving the European Union. It's getting boring now and I quickly get annoyed by the endless stream of pointless, pompous politicians giving their views on how they intend to block it. I decide to read the sports pages instead. At least there's a full weekend of football ahead. I can plan my weekend television around this – I'd intended to go to the gym today, but my muscles are far too sore for that. I might have to go tomorrow instead; curse Don, he's ruined my routine. These days I find it hard to train on consecutive days, that's the problem I've found in my forties; it's not that I'm weaker, I just take longer to recover and so I lose strength through training less often.

Despite myself, I take another quick look to see if Bella is online, but she isn't. My mind drifts again to what she might be doing if she's not chatting with me and whether it's something intimate with her husband. I imagine her cappuccino-coloured breasts heaving up and down as she rides him, bringing him to a climax. I like it when we do that, so he must like it too.

I can hear movement outside the door as floorboards creak. It sounds heavier than a twelve-year-old boy so it must be Maxine. I turn off my phone and place it on the table next to the bed. The usual routine now is for her to poke her head around the door and see if I want tea. So, I settle back down to a foetal position and pretend I'm still sleepy. I can hear the door gently creak open and I sense more light enter the room. I look up pseudo-sleepily and can see Maxine peer in through the doorway.

'Cup of tea?' she asks, gesturing with an invisible mug in her hand. I nod and stretch out my arms, turn to lie on my back and yawn, being careful not to strain my muscles any more than they already are.

'Yes please, that would be great,' I say. I can't remember the last time I made her a morning drink. I think she likes doing it, but I probably ought to offer to do it sometime. She disappears downstairs and I can hear the kettle being switched on. I take another look at my phone to see if Bella is online, but she isn't.

'Thanks,' I say as Maxine reappears with a hot mug of tea and places it on the table next to me with a digestive biscuit. She climbs into the bed, while I hear Jamie's footsteps nearby, now looking into the room from the doorway. He smiles at me, making an initial forward motion like he's about break into a run and then checks himself. He's becoming more self-aware, more restrained, cool, which is a shame.

'How's it going, Dad,' he says, strutting calmly towards the bed. I nod at him and smile.

'OK sunshine. How have you been?' He shrugs nonchalantly, but then pushes me into the middle of the bed as he snuggles up next to me. I shuffle along closer to Maxine to create some room, trying not to grimace at the pain coming from my aching body.

'So, what do you both want to do with the day?' I ask them as Jamie passes me my tea.

'Well, I have a few jobs to do on my list,' Maxine says. She starts to rattle off a range of household tasks that all sound hard work. Jamie looks at me and rolls his eyes, I smirk back at him and he laughs. Jamie will no doubt have his own plans for the day and have researched a bunch of things we could do together – all the movies showing at the cinema, live sports on TV or any latest releases we could stream.

'Got a game today?' I ask him. He plays football for his local team, although he's terrible. He shakes his head.

'There's a good movie on at 11 a.m. I would like to see though,' he says.

'Oh yes?' I say, acting surprised that he's suggested it.

'Well, there are various chores we need to do first before seeing any movie,' says Maxine true to form.

'Oh Mum!' he says.

'Like cleaning your room,' she says, and he shoots me another smile. I look down and I can see him mimicking a talking gesture with his hand as Maxine looks serious and continues to run off a list of even more chores for him. I wish she would go easier on him. Sometimes I feel she sees him as just being in the way.

'Well, if you want to go and see it, it sounds like you have some jobs to do first,' I say.

'OK, OK Mum, I'll do them!' His smile grows and he quickly wriggles himself out of bed to get started.

'Dad, you need to get up and showered,' he says as he runs out of the room. I take another sip of my tea.

'Oh I do, do I… ? ' I say. He pokes his head back in the doorway.

'Yes, you smell!' he says, running from the room before I can throw something at him.

Maxine stays in bed beside me and tells me what she has been doing for the week, the latest gossip from work and then lists the chores that I need to do. I restart my phone as she talks, taking a glance at the football news.

'Is there anything you want to do?' she asks, taking a moment to catch her breath.

'Hmm?'

'Jez, are you listening to me?' she says, sighing.

'Hmm?' I turn off my phone momentarily, but I am never entirely sure what she wants me to say at this point. Clearly, I am not listening, but I know that's not an answer she much likes.

'Oh, I don't mind. Maybe we could find time for a short walk?' I suggest. I swear if she had a tail it would wag.

'Great!' she says and carries on chatting, drinking her tea, telling some story of something that happened at work which she is greatly interested by. I conclude it's now safe to return my attention back to the sports news.

It approaches 10 a.m. and I've finished my tea. I'm gradually feeling more with it after yesterday's exertions. I'm not sure whether I really do smell after having had a late-night shower, but another in the morning does sound good to help loosen me up. Don is not ergonomically efficient or else you would see a lot of Don-shaped weights and objects in the gym for people to lift, but you don't. I guess that would also not be socially acceptable as most people don't have much reason to train their body to carry Don shapes around.

He was so heavy though. I imagine that's why some serial killers favour cutting people up. But this has never appealed to me; it's just so messy, why would you possibly want to do that? All those spilled bodily fluids would be a dream for a forensics team too, so unless the circumstances specifically demand it, I doubt I will be cutting up a body any time soon.

Maxine eventually stops talking and I agree to whatever it was that she last said.

'Great, so we're agreed then?' she says.

'Sure.'

The Present Tale

Bella works at Drake's and ideally I would see her this weekend. But I can't see how that will happen as we have no plans. I've tried to end things with her a few times over the last couple of years as although she is mostly perfect, she is also heavily conflicted. It can be very tiring to be around her. However, she is addictively dirty while also appearing extremely virtuous to anyone who doesn't know her. Her husband's alright – we've met a few times and I do feel some guilt about having sex with his wife, but not so much that I would stop. He's fairly poorly too, suffering a chronic health condition that she told me about, but I forget what it is. Not anything fatal, but something about always being fatigued, or was it laziness – I'm not sure. Either way she's his carer and unlikely to ever leave him.

I take another look at my phone to see if I have any messages, but I still haven't. Thinking about her all morning has made me feel aroused. I look at Maxine, still sitting next to me, and can see the outline of her breasts underneath her pyjama top. I turn my phone off and put an arm around her – she seems grateful for the attention and responds enthusiastically.

***

At 11 a.m. Jamie and I arrive at the cinema to see a thriller that he tells me has had great reviews. Maxine didn't fancy it and so didn't come. I'd put her behind on her housework schedule and so she stayed at home doing something else. Gardening, I think. I'm still not sure what chores I agreed to do for the day.

'Here's some money for popcorn, but you have to queue for it,' I say to Jamie.

'Oh Dad, can't you do it?' he asks, looking at me with puppy dog eyes.

'Nope. If you want it, you get it.' He takes the money from me and slopes off to join the back of the queue.

I see it as part of his development to stand and wait in line, learning the very British art of queuing. Besides, it frustrates the hell out of me to stand behind people who have no concept of time, or any awareness that other people actually want to see a movie. They are often enormous too, clutching all manner of snacks in their greedy fists. Wherever possible I try to avoid putting myself in a position where I have to mix with people like that. I look over at Jamie in the queue as I wait for him in the lobby. He's jumping up and down on the spot as he looks at his watch in a state of panic that the movie will soon start and then occasionally over to me. He never seems to realise there are endless trailers before the movie. I feel for my watch on my wrist but it isn't there – I must have forgotten to put it on this morning. I shrug back at him; it's better he's frustrated in the queue rather than me. Predictably, he's standing behind a very large couple and it looks as though they are ordering cappuccinos. Who orders cappuccinos at a cinema when there's only one cashier and a long line of people waiting to watch a movie? It is the epitome of selfishness. I should just walk up to them and slit their throats for being so ignorant, but would that be socially acceptable? I am generally a calm psychopath, especially when I'm not the one queuing in line. I prefer waiting to pick the right moment to commit murder and this isn't the time. Jamie turns to look over at me again, increasingly panicked. I gesture for him to calm down and wait, but in his agitated state he stumbles backwards into the fat man in front of him. The man spills his cappuccino over the counter, which makes me laugh, although he doesn't seem amused.

'Watch it kid,' I lip-read him saying. Jamie looks mortified, apologising profusely. But the fat man still looks angry and pushes him. I sigh and get up from my seat. Who pushes a kid for heaven's sake?

Settling down to watch the movie we have gained some free cappuccinos and a huge bag of sweets to keep us sustained.

'Dad, what did you say to that man?' asks Jamie.

'Nothing son, don't worry about it,' I say.

'No, but why did he leave the cinema?' he asks.

I shrug back.

'He realised it's not nice to push people, Jamie.'

'OK,' he says. I feel him nestle his head gently against my shoulder. It feels like when he was little boy, and I smell his head. It's the same as when he was a baby.

The trailers start and I have one final check of my phone before I have to fully turn it off. I see that I now have a message waiting from Bella. I feel like ignoring it, it's so late, but despite myself I open it.

Hey! How is your morning?

I ponder whether to reply instantly or wait a while. I turn my phone off and decide she can wait for a response until after the movie.

Two hours later, Jamie and I come out of the cinema. 'What did you think Dad, did you like it? I loved it. I think Mark Wahlberg is great you know; he makes such good movies. Do you think I could be like him one day? I've been thinking about what I want to do for a career and I think being a CIA agent would suit me down to the ground,' he says. Kids are so impressionable. I wonder if I took him to see a movie about a lovable serial killer whether he would want to be one.

'Uh huh,' I say. At least it's a bit more realistic than being a Jedi, which had been his career plan until about a year ago. Less time swishing lightsabers and more time practising football skills would have been a profitable use of time. He continues talking about the movie while I check the time on my phone and I see it's approaching lunch.

'Fancy a pizza?' I ask. He starts jumping up and down on the spot again.

'Yes, please!'

'It's just a pizza, Jamie.'

'Pizza is my favourite.'

'Really?' I ask sarcastically.

'Yes, Dad. It comes from Italy and they make the best pizzas over there you know; it comes down to the freshness of the ingredients and them making the dough with locally milled flour. Our teacher said that since the 1980s the commercialisation of mass fast food outlets has increased our awareness of different cultures, but this has also diminished the quality of overall food standards.'

'Fascinating Jamie, just fascinating,' I say as I play with my phone while we walk to the local Pizza Bar. I text Maxine to let her know we won't be back until mid-afternoon. Chores will have to wait. I look back over in his direction and realise he's still talking about pizzas. I'm not convinced Pizza Bar source their flour locally, nor indeed even make their pizza bases in the restaurant.

My phone pings as Maxine texts back:

OK, you boys have fun

She has added a few emoji kisses. I hate emojis.

At Pizza Bar, Jamie talks continuously for an hour between bites of his pizza. It must be something to have such an inquisitive mind where you are fascinated by all sorts of mundane things. I decide to check in with Bella over text while he carries on. My phone pings back instantly this time:

Maybe I could come and accidently bump into you both if you are in town?

I reply:

OK, but you will need to get here soon

But as I read the next message I see she's changed her mind almost as quickly as she made it and I groan out loud. Jamie looks up, momentarily distracted from his chatter.

Oh I think Mike will be suspicious if I left now though

I wonder why I ever bother with these discussions.

*If we had planned a bit earlier, then it would be less of a
rush now*

I text my reply as I put my phone down, intent on not
messaging further, but then it immediately pings again so
I pick it back up.

Yes, yes I know. Sorry about that. Sorry to let you down

I don't ask what she was doing this morning to prevent her
texting earlier.

Leaving the restaurant, I glance at my phone before I
put it in my pocket. I can see there are twenty messages. I
just scroll to the last one.

It's not that I don't want to be with you

I could scream, I really could. I decide to delete all twenty.
What a creature of contradiction she is; it was only a week
ago she was lap dancing me to Sade's 'Smooth Operator'.

The Tale of the Bank

End

I check my watch and see it's now 7.20 a.m. I pick up the binoculars again, but decide it's just paranoia that's making me want to take another look at Leighton's house. I will arouse suspicion if I keep doing that and I need to remain incognito. Suddenly I'm startled as my phone vibrates. I fumble in my pocket for it. This is not what need I right now; I look on the screen and see it's Maxine.

'Hello?' I say, deciding it's best to take the call.

'Hi sweetie, what are you up to?' she says. She's never fully lost her stalking nature, so I look around me to see if she is nearby, but I can't see any sign of her.

'Oh not much,' I say. 'Just in the car, taking a break before getting to campus.'

'Still tired? Poor baby,' she says, although it sounds like she doesn't believe me. It's uncanny how she can sniff out when I'm up to something.

'A little bit,' I say. I didn't sleep too well last night and she could sense I was restless, I woke her a couple of times when I visited the bathroom. As ever, she was attentive and rapidly on hand with offers of cups of tea. She didn't know my restlessness was excitement at the thought of finally paying Leighton a visit.

Leighton has been a festering sore for years. Maxine

has never really gotten over what happened and frankly it's getting to the point where I'm fed up with her mentioning him. I see today as a means of righting a wrong, also shutting her up about it, although I can't ever tell her of this. So it'll be my quiet duty to get rid of him. Of course I also disliked Leighton for humiliating me as a junior banker, so I can't say I'm entirely selfless. But after he took sexual advantage of Maxine it feels as though I have a justifiable reason for an honour killing. It's a strangely nice feeling that I'm doing some good too; almost like charity work. I've kept an eye on his whereabouts for years, loosely monitoring his career, being careful not to be detected, nor to be in his vicinity, just watching. He stayed at the Abingdon branch for three more years after I left, which meant he was there with Maxine for another six months before she moved to Sheffield. I don't know how many sexual favours she gave him or indeed whether it even happened again – what I do know is she cried about it so I couldn't tolerate that for ever. Sooner or later I would need to pay him a visit.

When Maxine transferred to the Sheffield city branch of the bank it had surprised me. She called me up one day to ask me to see her for lunch in Sheffield – I thought she was just visiting for the day, but she'd actually moved. She looked so lost and forlorn, I didn't know whether to be angry with her or be pleased to see her. In a practical sense it was handy as she had a full-time salary with disposable income which I certainly did not have as a student. So life became a bit easier and more comfortable, although I soon felt constantly monitored.

Initially she stayed in a women's hostel while she settled in but when she needed to leave there, I said she could stay in my student digs for a while until she got sorted. I only had a single bed, a black and white TV and was managing on a diet of Pot Noodles and tinned curry. But she loved being there, making it all homely. We hadn't even regularly slept together, just occasionally, and only ever at the end of an evening after I had already struck out with someone else. She was always on hand and willing to please. As it turns out she had surprisingly effective skills that I hadn't expected and it both excited and revolted me that Leighton had been with her, too.

I try to get Maxine off the phone, but she's persistent and it can be tricky to shake her off without upsetting her; she would detect something is up and track me down. 'Was there something you wanted?' I ask.

'No, not really, just wondering how your morning was going,' she says. It was only an hour ago I was with her at her father's house in Abingdon.

'We've spoken about this,' I say. She agreed, as part of our marriage pact, that she would let me get on with life a bit more and I promised that Tommy was an isolated incident that he had initiated, not me. Marriage was the only solution, apart from killing her – and that seemed mean; a bit like killing Lassie. I should buy her a pet when we get to Australia. That will occupy her.

'Yes, I know. I'm a bit excited about Australia I guess. Should I buy some new clothes for the weather there?' she says.

'Better wait till you are there?'

'OK.'

'Can I go now?' I ask, feeling a little agitated as I glance again at my wrist-watch.

'Angry with me?'

'No.'

'Can you pick up some milk?'

'Fine.'

'Be careful Jez, promise me?' she says. I pause for a moment. Surely she doesn't know what I'm doing.

'I'll get the milk,' I say.

'OK.'

Finally freeing myself from the call, I take another glance through the binoculars at Leighton's house. There's no sign of anyone yet. It's a pleasant looking, large, detached house in a leafy suburb of Abingdon. He had evidently done well after leaving the local branch to go to the Oxford headquarters. Leighton became the regional business manager for the South East of England. So that's excellent progress for a rapist, although his run of good fortune is about to come to an end.

From my ad hoc surveillance of his movement patterns I thought some time after the morning school run would work best to get to him. In recent weeks Mondays and Fridays seemed the best opportunities to catch him on his own, although on Mondays his movement seems more unpredictable than Fridays. On Fridays his wife tends to drop their teenage daughter off at school before he leaves the house. So Friday is a late start for him, often up to 11 a.m. or 12 p.m. He is also the last person on the street to leave for work on Fridays, so I should have some privacy with him. From where I now sit, I can see just one other house facing directly on to his, but the couple who live there don't appear to have children and are away before 7.30 a.m. sharing a single vehicle. As I glance again, I can see them closing their front door behind them now. It's 7.35 a.m. and so, although they are a little behind today, all remains on schedule.

I have a while to wait now and so I start to play with the gadgets on the car. Nissans tend to come with quite high specifications for a competitive price, so I'm impressed. This one seems to have a heated driver's seat that will even vibrate gently if I want it to. I want it to.

I look at my watch, it's 8 a.m. and any time now Leighton's wife should emerge from their house closely followed by their daughter. She often returns to the house having forgotten something and then the mum gestures to her impatiently from the car, pointing to her watch.

It is 8.01 a.m. and their Oxford blue front door swings open, Leighton's wife Hilda strides out, grappling with a shoulder bag and pressing her car's remote fob device with her right hand to unlock it. There's no sign of their daughter yet as Hilda enters the car, places her bag on the back seat and buckles up. A minute passes and she starts the engine, looking impatient. There's still no sign of their daughter and although I expect her to be a bit late it causes me some anxiety as this could throw off the schedule. She looked around sixteen years old on my previous visits and it's plausible she could have a study day. I hadn't properly considered that. If that proves the case, I'm not sure what I will do about it as this really is his day of destiny. Killing his daughter along with him seems disproportionate, indulgent even. Ordinarily I might come back another day, but I'm running out of opportunities now as Australia awaits.

8.05 a.m. now and Hilda is backing out of the drive, still with no sign of their daughter. It looks like I will have to adapt and take both father and daughter, which makes me a bit uncomfortable. I would like to stick to the plan if possible and this carries risk. Taking two people instead of one would not pose undue physical challenge to me as I spent most of my university years in the gym and rowing, so I am quite athletic now. No longer a skinny teenager, I took my weights sessions with Trevor seriously and even after Lorraine cheated on him, he stayed in contact with me, training me further. He was alright in the end – too good for her. I often check myself out in the mirror and know I've maintained my shape pretty well over the years. I'm easily far too much of a physical specimen for an out of shape fifty-something-year-old bank manager and his daughter.

I look in my kill kit and wonder if I've brought enough parcel tape for the two of them. I'm not sure, but I will just have to make it stretch a bit. You only need one baseball bat to batter two people so that would work – I could use it like a tennis racquet, operating forehand and backhand to take them both out simultaneously.

As I drift off into my imagination, playing the Wimbledon of serial kills with their heads, I hear Hilda toot her horn. She looks angry now and is shouting out of the driver's window towards the house. 'Hilary!' she screams at the top of her voice and I hear it all the way over in my car. How narcissistic of Hilda to call her daughter Hilary. I bet if they had a son he would be Lenton.

Hilary flies out of the door, slamming it behind her and at the same time asking her mum to quieten down with a downwards hand gesture. She looks every bit the stroppy teenager. As she gets closer to the car I can see through my binoculars she is mouthing some expletives to her mother. Teenagers, bless them.

Over the next ten minutes the rest of the cul-de-sac empties of vehicles and I tick them off my list, using the clipboard I have now perched on the steering wheel. None of the drivers pay me any attention – that's the advantage of using a Nissan Micra, it just blends into the background. Sitting in the driver's seat I'm now wearing a baseball cap coupled with blue overalls that I think make me look like a convincing delivery man. This outfit was a decent purchase from a fancy-dress shop in Cardiff a couple of years ago, although quite who goes to fancy-dress parties dressed like this is beyond me. Perhaps it's mostly worn by strippers, or for the benefit of bored housewives with a fetish for delivery men. It'll do the job if anyone sees me on the street and I have the baseball bat next to me ready for action. I already know it fits neatly down the back of my jacket and on exiting the car I'll put it in place, tucking it into the back of my pants to secure it. I can also draw it with reasonable speed from over my left shoulder with my right hand. Kind of like a samurai from a Japanese movie. Doing this one handed also means I can still hold my clipboard too.

Time rolls on to 9 a.m. and there's still no sign of Leighton. So his pattern is holding and he's having a late start, which is good. It's probably his paperwork morning, which is a strategy that works for me too. It's a good opportunity to catch up on all those nagging jobs I haven't been able to get to all week. I start to feel twitchy about whether I should make my move now as I need to be careful to time this and also make sure I don't miss my opportunity when everything else seems to be falling so well into place. I can feel excitement build but I know I must stay calm and focused.

It's 9.01 a.m. and so I slip a CD into the Nissan's music system to get me in the right mood. As it fires up, I take a deep breath, clutch the bat, my holdall and the clipboard. It'll soon be time to get the show on the road and for this special occasion I've selected The Soup Dragons, 'Soft As Your Face', as Leighton's theme song. Why 'Soft As Your Face' – it's a weak joke I know, but I'm going to enjoy pulverising Leighton's face and somehow it seems apt. It'll be soft alright when I'm finished – like a good schnitzel. What strong and vivid memories my private song selection brings to me. It feels good to know The Soup Dragons will join my playlist – that song should have been a massive hit, one of those undiscovered gems. I think I might even make a call into a radio station tomorrow, a request for the song, dedicated to the memory of Leighton. How poignant it will be; people might like that – perhaps his wife will hear it and then remember the song too. These little mementos really are terrific and one day I will have assembled the top forty of my greatest hits; although I have some way to go yet. When I'm old, immobile and no longer able to properly enjoy my hobby, I'll be able to sit quietly with a hot chocolate, listening to my favourite music and reminiscing over happy days. Songs also get me in the right mood too, keep me focused and give me some rhythm. So as I close the car door behind me, I groove along the street towards the house, with the tune fresh in my mind, singing to myself.

'For every word you speak is tongue in cheek and tongue in cheek is tongue out of place…,' I sing, skipping down the street in a thoroughly good mood.

As I get within 100 metres of the house, I am on the

second chorus, thinking of how I will obliterate Leighton's face with a baseball bat.

'For I go crazy, I go as soft as your face, as soft as your face.'

At this moment Leighton chooses to exit the front door, which startles me so I stop singing. He looks rushed and thankfully he doesn't notice me, but I can see he's red in the face. Looking at him, closer than usual, I can see he's put on a few pounds over the years. His choice in suits hasn't improved – it may even be the same one he wore back in the day.

He dives into his car, closes the driver's door behind him and starts the engine. It looks like he's off to work earlier than normal. I stand still in my tracks, almost 100 metres from him. It's not handy to my plan if he drives to work. The sound of his Mercedes starting is the sound of a quality vehicle revving into life. I will give him that, he might have a poor choice of suit but he does have a nice car. The Mercedes reverses a few metres down his driveway but then suddenly stops. He gets out, looks even redder in the face and slams the driver's door behind him. He doesn't look happy and walks around to the rear of the car. I can see him bending down now and examining the rear tyre on the driver's side and then the others. He stands back up scratching his head, then glances at his watch and delivers a stiff kick to the nearest tyre which makes me laugh – it was clearly a worthwhile exercise to pre-emptively let them all down this morning.

Having evidently decided it is impossible to change all four tyres himself, I watch as he returns to his house and notice he is already fishing in his pocket for his mobile phone. On reflection, I hadn't fully considered what might happen if he's on the phone when he sees me? If he recognises me or calls out my name I could be in trouble. So I decide I'll give him a couple of minutes to make his call before I knock on the door.

Waiting a few minutes, I decide to proceed, so I recommence humming about his soft face and then sidle over to the front door. My heart is beating faster than I thought it would so the song becalms me, getting me in the right 'zone.'

'For I go crazy, I go as soft as your face…'

I reach his car and look down at his flat tyres. There's almost no air in them at all. I adjust my gloves, make sure my sunglasses and cap are firmly in place to avoid him immediately recognising me and stride towards the door.

I manage to draw the bat from over my shoulder in one smooth movement. Clearing my throat, I ring the doorbell and follow up with a rapid, firm knock on the door to be sure. Sometimes people do not change the batteries in their doorbells, so I do not want to be left hanging here too long. There is no immediate answer, so I knock again. All is quiet for a moment but then I hear a familiar voice.

'Coming. Hang on a minute,' he says. It's the same gruff voice I recognise from my banking days and vivid thoughts of him flood back to me. I feel rage begin to rise in me as I hear the latch.

'I go crazy…' I hum along and then see the door swing open. He's not on the phone, but looks perplexed for a moment, wondering what's happening as he sizes me up and down.

'You called for some new tyres?' I say. He looks puzzled.

'No I didn't... ' he protests, still looking quizzical, not understanding what's happening and then spying the baseball bat in my right hand which I can see confuses him. But I quickly push the base of my foot into his stomach and he stumbles backwards into the house. I latch the door behind us.

'What the hell do you want?' he asks, stumbling to his feet. I don't say anything, but as he stands I drop the clipboard I'm holding to the floor, put both hands on the baseball bat, raise it back over my shoulder and then forward, smashing it into his right knee. He screams in pain and falls to the ground. 'Please, just take what you want,' he says.

It feels like a movie scene and this excites me. Everything happens in slow-motion and I take in the surroundings. The moment is everything I hoped it would be – I've waited a long time for this and it's not a disappointment. I wish it would never end and so I carry on singing to myself. I feel impregnable, immortal and that I have all the time in the world to do exactly as I wish. I suck in a deep breath through my nostrils to savour the smell, the finer details, committing everything to memory, looking at their cute family portrait on the sideboard, the stripes of the wallpaper, and the smell of fresh toast still in the air from breakfast.

I look down and see Leighton writhing on the floor, clutching his knee. He doesn't seem sure whether to be submissive in the hope I'll take pity and go away, or whether he should try to launch a counterattack. But I'm hovering over him with a baseball bat in my hands and he thinks better of it. I decide to immediately remove the possibility of him trying anything by smashing another blow into him with the bat. This time to his right arm and I hear his humerus bone break. What a 'crack' it makes – that's got to be broken in a few places. He vomits onto the carpet and curls up into a ball, pleading for me not to hurt him further. But for safety of mind I need to fully disable him and remove all possibility of getting into a tussle. Tussles mean physical contact and the risk of leaving my DNA under his nails or on his body, so I take a backhand swing from left to right, this time aiming at his left arm, and I hear that crack too. It's a softer noise this time – my backhand always was a bit off. He doesn't change his position but is crying like a baby now. I figure I've done enough to remove any immediate threat, but I turn to the hall table and disconnect the telephone. I can't see his mobile phone anywhere, so I stay vigilant, watching him. I wait for a while until his pain levels normalise and he gets used to his new equilibrium. Once he starts to calm, he'll be able to concentrate better and understand what's happening. There's no point chatting with him like this, screaming. It's a good job all his neighbours are out.

It takes a while but after some minutes he realises I'm no longer swinging the bat and he uncoils slightly to face me. I can see saliva and remnants of vomit dripping from his lower lip.

'Please… ' he says.

'It's a bit late for please,' I say. I remove my sunglasses and he squints at me, trying to get a closer look. His glasses have fallen off and are lying on the floor near him. I can see where they are but I don't think he can. I'm not going to touch them.

'I know you, don't I?' he says. I smirk at him as he squints harder at me.

'Yes, you do,' I say. I leave it with him to make the connection. It also seems appropriate in this circumstance to appear enigmatic, kind of like an evil Clint Eastwood. If anyone ever wanted to make a film of this, I would look cool, maybe classy even. Although if I was properly thinking of this as a movie, I could probably have done better than wearing blue overalls. Who could play me? I bet Brad Pitt is too busy.

'Jeremy?' he asks, mumbling nervously. 'Is that you Jeremy? It is you, isn't it?'

'Yes, Leighton. How have you been? It's been a while.' I stay standing facing him. My attempt at humour has blown my Clint tough guy persona and the familiarity seems to have perversely emboldened him with aggression. I should have stayed in character but then I guess he wouldn't know it's me. A catch-22 situation for sure.

'What the hell are you doing, Jeremy? Stop this nonsense immediately – why would you do this?'

'Think back Leighton, why do you think I am here?' I say.

'If this is about how I mentored you – I was only ever cruel to be kind, you know. I never meant it personally. I'm sorry if I upset you, but this is no way to act.' He looks at me as he tries to get up stumbling on to his good knee, wincing as his right knee touches the floor. I think I must have cracked his kneecap too. That's got to hurt and I wince sympathetically. I'm not a monster.

'You were a complete bastard, Leighton, and you have had this coming for a long time,' I say.

'You're going to get into so much trouble over this, Jeremy. Leave now before it's too late. You can't just burst into people's houses and assault them. You will go to prison for this, you mark my words. I just don't understand whatever has possessed you.' He's trying to stand now but I sweep his left leg away and he falls down again. He screams out in pain.

'Do you remember Maxine?' I ask him as he writhes on the floor. He's not properly listening. 'Maxine. Who is now my wife. Do you recall what you did to her?' I ask.

'Maxine? Yes of course I remember her. You married her? Oh my god, really? You married her?'

'Do you remember what you did to her and why that might mean I'm now here to visit you?' I ask, taking the moral high ground. He will see he deserves this now I'm quite sure.

'I have no idea what you are talking about,' he says dismissively.

'Careful Leighton, do you want me to smash your other arm?'

'No, please don't do that. Yes I do remember now. I'm sorry but she propositioned me,' he says.

'I doubt that,' I say.

'It wasn't me! I was shocked, but I was also weak at a terrible time in my marriage and she told me she would pay off her overdraft with sex. Forgive me, Jeremy, but I was weak!' he says.

'That's not how she describes events. She tells a very different story, one where you forced her.' I raise my bat again. He looks at me pleadingly.

'Please, Jeremy. It was her idea. I was just weak. Forgive

me for being weak,' he says. It wasn't quite the answer I was expecting, but I've heard enough of this now and time is racing on. I take a big back lift, making sure to bend my knees for best ergonomic effect, and swing the bat at his head this time, and I don't stop until he's no longer moving. That swing would have been a home run for sure. He looks quite the mess – as soft as your face indeed. I take a small baggie of cocaine out of my pocket, sprinkle some over him and then empty most of it onto the carpet next to his glasses. That'll confuse the police.

As I take a last look around the scene to check for loose ends, I catch a glance at myself in the mirror. I could do with losing a few pounds too – my cheekbones are not as prominent as they should be. I need to revisit that low carbohydrate diet I tried a while ago. Blood splatter is not a good look either but at least it's his, not mine. As far as I can see, I don't seem to have left anything, so I adjust my cap down over my face, put my glasses back on, slowly unlatch the door and let myself out. Walking to the car I keep my head down, get in, start the engine and head out of the suburbs. I'll abandon the car, clean up, get rid of this uniform and change into my jogging gear. I'd better make a start on losing those excess pounds before we head off to Australia.

The Present Tale

Back home after the cinema trip with Jamie and now full up on pizza, I happily relax on the living room couch with the newspaper, pleased to have some time to myself. Tomorrow I will need to double-check my handiwork in the woods, but for now, relaxation is needed and as I read through the paper I see nothing about a body in the woods which is reassuring. I'd dug a pretty deep hole, so it's good that effort was well spent and didn't lead to an immediate discovery. You often hear of a body being found in a shallow grave, but less often from a deep one. I mean it's just obvious, isn't it, so if you really don't want to be discovered it's important to take the extra time to do things properly. Note to self and other serial killers – dig a deep hole.

When either Don's family or the university report him missing, things will get more interesting. Like when they find his car and the suicide note he left in it. The note was a nice touch, but it took him a little while to agree to write it. In the end he really didn't fancy a second blast from the Taser and resigned himself to his fate. It was either that or the threat to kill his wife and family. He was almost noble in the end, writing it to save them.

One of the things I think people don't often appreciate when they argue with a psychopath is how far a psychopath is prepared to go. I can't speak for 'normal' folk, but I certainly believe I can talk for my psychopath brethren. Most people genuinely feel everyone is like them and that's a *big* mistake. Assuming normal rules exist in an argument is very naive – what if you faced someone like me? It would not end well for you. If you argue with a psychopath, you should back off, it's that simple.

I decided long ago I wasn't going to let annoyance build up in me to the point where I felt the need to explode. Exploding with rage leads to imperfect decision-making and the strong likelihood of discovery. I don't intend to spend my life in prison, so I need to be a bit smarter than that. My anger needs an outlet and from time to time I need to hurt someone, but I'm socially aware enough to know it's unacceptable to bludgeon someone to death. Of course, I may be thinking about doing exactly that while at the same time smiling politely, planning a time when I can do it. But at least I will be smiling; I'm not some caricature psycho killer with horns and a menacing grin. Just don't misread the smile as friendliness. This principle of waiting, biding my time, has served me well and for a serial killer, I maintain a healthy balance in life. Otherwise, my body count would be much higher than it is. I even think my portfolio of work is probably at the middle to low end of the serial killer spectrum. I'm probably barely in the club at all really – if there was a club. I should start one, but then it would get all competitive like with Tommy.

The Present Tale

The rest of Saturday had flown by and I don't really do anything except watch TV and drink whisky until comatose so I can numb the Don-induced pain I'm feeling from my sore muscles. As I come downstairs early on Sunday morning, I'm feeling a little better. I can see the jeans I was wearing yesterday are on the arm of one of the sofas. I have no recollection of putting them there. That was a whole evening which simply passed me by in an alcoholic stupor. My dad would be so proud. I pick my phone out of the jeans pocket and think about looking to see if I have any messages from Bella. I don't want to look though and slip it straight into my pocket.

Jamie's in the living room munching on some toast and he looks over in my direction momentarily before refocusing his gaze on some football programme playing on TV. I really wish he was a better player but at least he seems to enjoy himself.

Maxine pops her head around the living room door. 'Do you fancy a coffee?' she asks. I nod and she goes back to the kitchen. I can hear her humming happily as she boils the kettle.

'What's the live game on TV today?' I ask Jamie.

'Liverpool vs Newcastle at midday.'

'Oh great,' I say, settling in and curling myself up on the sofa. Maxine brings us both drinks and a small plate of biscuits. Sunday is normally an annoyingly short day for me as I either must travel back to USL in Ormskirk late in the afternoon or else drive straight there early on Monday morning. Neither are great options and I'm growing to dislike the journey. It was all so much easier when I worked nearby at Drake's, but you can only work at a low-ranked institute for so long before you become permanently associated with it. My thoughts turn to Don and I smile to myself thinking of him now settled in his woodland home. It must be peaceful there – squirrels, birds, worms. He wouldn't like the worms I guess.

Jamie and I watch the game together, Liverpool win 2-1 so we are both happy, except I can't really have a drink because I've decided to drive back to Ormskirk later. We both follow Liverpool. Why did I choose Liverpool? Because my uncle Jeff once asked me as a young kid who I supported.

'Who's top of the league?' I remember asking.

'Liverpool,' said Uncle Jeff.

'That's my team!' I said. So that was that and I've been a Liverpool fan ever since.

As I relax after the game, I remember there were a few messages I'd missed from Bella. I take my phone out of my pocket to have a look.

Are you OK or are you angry with me?

This one from 7 a.m. this morning. Another one at 8.15 a.m.

Come on, I wasn't that neurotic

And another at 9.04 a.m.

Sorry OK, just text me?

She really is neurotic. I think she gets off on it, but maybe that's also why she's been getting away with seeing me in secret so long – she's super careful. Her husband's not stupid either. Bella would deny her neurosis, but I think it feeds her Catholic guilt complex.

Hi, all OK here

I type, wanting to appear happy-go-lucky in the message although that's very far from how I feel. Unsurprisingly, she's not live on WhatsApp, or at least not during the fifteen minutes that I'm online, and I can see my message remains unread. She can really irritate me with her moral values. She's had sex with me maybe over a hundred times in all kinds of ways and she's still guilty about it every time.

I have a shower, get dressed and realise I didn't go for a walk with Maxine yesterday after all. I must have drunk far too much. I should take her out today, but I also need to get a gym session done. I ask her if she wants to take a walk into town and if so, I can multi-task the trip by getting in a quick workout while she goes for a coffee or shopping. She seems happy with that idea, keen to spend time together.

The Present Tale

Sunday evening and the weekend has gone so fast, but thankfully my muscles are now less sore after my exertions on Friday. It's not every week you Taser, suffocate and bury your former boss in a deeply dug grave in the woods. So it's been an eventful weekend and this gives me plenty to reflect upon as I prepare to undertake the two-hour drive from home.

I find the key to being a killer is having a thorough plan and yet be adaptable. I'd been surprised by the janitor so that was sloppy, but I was a bit rushed and nevertheless coped quite well. In my fledgling days of being a killer I might have been more thrown by that and it's possible the janitor might have had to join my collection. Until this recent adventure with Don, I have always been very careful.

The Tale of Being Neighbourly

Australian Summer, 2010

Now happily living in Australia, with Leighton long since dealt with, I'm packing a suitcase ready for a well-deserved Christmas vacation in New Zealand. The phone rings and I can see it's Maxine's mobile number. She does not have good news.

'What do you mean we can't go on holiday?' I say. She was only popping in to see the doctor for a check-up. This will be the first holiday we've had since moving to Australia. I had to prioritise getting established as Head of the Business School of Janszoon University and then Jamie was born so I became even busier. He's a nice kid, but children and flights are not a good mix in my opinion. I've been sat close to enough screaming children over the years to know that. But this is a much-needed holiday.

'The doctor says he thinks I might have breast cancer,' says Maxine. It sounds like she's crying. I sigh and stop folding my Ted Baker chinos for a moment.

'Can't this wait until we get back? We're only going to be away for a week,' I say. I'm trying to be reasonable, but I don't think she realises how expensive the trip to New Zealand is. I doubt I'll be able to get a refund if we don't go. I wait for her to answer, but she doesn't say anything, all I can hear is some stifled sniffing on the other end of the phone.

'Jez, please… ' she says.

'Can you just ask if we can get straight back onto it when we get back from the holiday? That's all I am saying.' Surely the doctor can see the sense in that and a week's holiday will help her, I'm sure of it. Besides, back in the UK the NHS waiting times would be much longer than this, so I can't see the need to rush treatment.

'I'll ask,' says Maxine eventually. Relieved, I put her on speaker-phone so I can restart packing.

I hear mumbled chatter and then a male voice in the background, presumably the doctor. There's a loud cough and then he comes on to the phone.

'I think you had better come down to the surgery for a conversation,' he says, pompously.

'Fine,' I say. I put the phone down and look at my watch. I realise I should have encouraged her to go to the doctor's after the trip in case it was anything serious. I clearly did not think that through, but she only had a blotchy rash across one breast – there was no lump. I assumed she was just fighting an infection and he might give her some antibiotics to tide her over for a week.

At the doctor's surgery, the receptionist looks like she has anticipated my arrival and waves me straight through to the consultation room. She has a very severe look, her hair's in a tight bun, but she's still not an unattractive woman – middle-aged. I presume she's trained to look severe and I wonder what she might look like in a black PVC catsuit, holding a whip. I knock on the consulting room door and enter.

Thirty minutes later and the holiday is officially off.

Maxine is quiet in the car on the way back and so she should be – this is going to cost a fortune. The doctor was pretty rude to me and so I don't think that helped the situation. I stayed calm under his provocation, even though I will now need to get in touch with the insurers to make the best of it and try to get some sort of a refund.

'Jez, I'm so sorry,' says Maxine. That's considerate of her so I pat her on the knee – it's not really her fault I guess, although the trip did take a lot of planning.

'It's OK, Maxine,' I say, reassuringly. Although as I look at her, I do think she could have waited for the appointment. She seems to like the pats on her knee and puts her hand on top of mine.

As we pull up into our driveway and wait for our electric garage door to open, I can already hear the irritating noise of music from our noisy bogan neighbour, Jason, as it screeches from the stereo in his garage.

'That bloody idiot,' I say and Maxine mumbles something in agreement through her handkerchief. I look over in his direction before driving into the garage. He's only been here six months and has quickly become an annoying presence. His constant music, beer swilling and informal male-bonding gatherings on his driveway are becoming the new normal.

'Bogan asshole,' I say which makes Maxine laugh a little. Bogans are much like British chavs. He constantly wears board shorts and a vest to show off his tattoos, even though he doesn't have the defined muscles needed to make bicep tattoos work. Why do people do that – if you have puny arms, tattoos don't make you look tough. He has a droopy hipster moustache and an uneven haircut you get from a barber who has been wading through a long queue. I use a stylist.

The other neighbours are drawn to him by the sight of his boat and trailer. I think they all hope he'll take them out for a daytrip to the reef one day, so he's rapidly become popular on the street. But, of course, they don't have to live next door to him, and months of music pulsing through the walls of the house is really annoying. I've spoken with him about the noise before and he called me a 'fussy pommy bastard'. I just smiled back at him, thinking how I would like to skewer him through his anus with a fishing harpoon and then use it to roast him on a spit. It will come to a head again soon enough as he's taken to intentionally turning up the music whenever he sees us now.

'I think I need to rest,' says Maxine. It has all been a bit of a shock for her, but I don't think she has fully comprehended how this will impact on me at all yet. But that's OK, she's allowed to be a bit selfish. We can talk about that later. The doctor said he wants her to start chemotherapy tomorrow and what with it being Christmas Eve, the traffic will be appalling. We were supposed to be on a plane for our holidays – why does this shit happen to *me*.

'Yes sure, understandable,' I say and walk with her through to the bedroom. 'I'll pick up Jamie from day care.'

'That's very kind Jez, thank you,' she says as she gets undressed and heads to bed.

'No problem, you get some rest,' I say. I can still hear Jason's music pulsing through the wall, even though it's only midday. For now, I need to make some calls to the insurers and see what I can do about the holiday. I'll probably end up in a long queue to some call centre.

The Present Tale

As a pro-vice-chancellor for Research at USL, I've done quite well as an academic. But 'quite well' doesn't cut it with someone as competitive as me. It hasn't been easy to get this far and I've had to take some steps others might find unpalatable, but I would also say that in some form or another, academia is full of people very similar to me. I mean it's packed with them. I imagine I could walk down a corridor of any university campus at any moment and come across at least one person with some kind of antisocial personality disorder. Assuming of course they bother coming in to work at all – lazy bastards. That's probably what drew me to this world, the knowledge that I'm among like-minded people. This truly is the perfect place for me: full of narcissists, sociopaths and a scattering of true psychopaths willing to do anything to get ahead, just like me.

The sociopathic tendencies of academics quickly became apparent to me early in my career. Every one of them would push you out of the way to get ahead, some would shove, some nudge, some would throw you aside, and a few might just stab you to death. Relatively few are in the latter category and so this makes me feel special. Like a prince in a court. I am not yet the king, but I'm capable one day of taking the throne as a vice-chancellor, although at the moment I'm still a few places away from succession.

A few years ago, I did a management training course with the whole of the senior leadership team and my personality type came out identical to our vice-chancellor. Both of us made the course trainers very nervous, recognising what we were – I saw the sweat develop on the top lip of the session leader. It made me want to slice it off her face for glimpsing the real me, but the vice-chancellor found it all hilarious, which took the edge off the moment. She took me under her wing after that too, at least until she did what leaders do – screw it all up and then leave. I found our similarity to be vindication that I was destined to be a vice-chancellor myself and so this became my goal. So it's not usual practice for me to kill vice-chancellors. Don was the exception; just a sweaty little man who tried to blackmail my mistress into sleeping with him.

The Present Tale

My mobile phone rings on the drive back to my flat on Sunday evening. It's Bella.

'You heard the news?' she says.

'No, what's up?' I ask. She sounds out of breath as if she'd been running, or maybe having sex. She isn't a runner so in my mind I become convinced she's been screwing her husband.

'Don's missing – it's on the news now.' I realise now what she's talking about. I allow myself to smirk at my handiwork.

'Oh really, what happened?' I ask, doing my best to sound surprised. She can never know what I've done, or that I did it for her. I don't think she would understand.

'Search parties are looking for him in the water off Southport Pier,' she says.

'That doesn't sound good. It can be rough water around there,' I say.

'Yes, not much hope if he's in the water,' she says. It sounds like she's upset, although her breathing rate is recovering now. This is the cycle she goes through after sex; first breathless and worn out, panting and then slowly, regaining her composure. It's very cute to observe and right now I'm distracted thinking of it.

'Why was he in the water? Did he fall?' I ask.

'Just listening now. Sounds like it might be intentional,' she says.

'Intentional?' I ask.

'They're saying there was a note. Suicide I think,' she says.

'Ah, OK. What a shame.' I say, doing my best to sound sympathetic.

'Well, not really a shame when he was pressuring me, I guess. Jez – is it very awful of me to be relieved he's dead?' she asks, sounding anxious now.

'No, not all. He was terrible – but he probably had other problems too if he was capable of suicide.'

'Yes I guess so,' she says. She pauses for a moment. 'Do you think they'll go through his phone? They might ask me about the texts he sent me. It would be awful if they asked me about them. What on earth would Mike think?'

'Did you respond to them?' I ask. She goes silent for a moment and it makes me wonder if she'd ever been with him. I feel a bit nauseous. He'd been known as 'Chasey Chaucer' for a reason.

'I only responded politely,' she says.

'I doubt he would be stupid enough to keep provocative texts on his phone,' I say. Anyone with a modicum of intelligence would have deleted them after sending them anyway. I looked through his phone when I had him incapacitated to check how she had responded to him. I didn't find any trace of messages between them.

As I arrive at my flat, Bella continues to give me a full account of the news coverage across the different channels, but all I can think about is her breathless voice, and vivid images flood into my mind of her panting, exhausted and sweaty on top of me and I wish she were with me now.

'Can you help me with something?' I ask her as I settle

back into the flat and unzip my trousers.

'Help with what?' she asks.

'You know what,' I say.

'No I can't!' she says, indignantly but also with laughter in her voice. 'You're incorrigible.'

Afterwards, I browse through the media to read about Don. Police have found his car and suicide note, but there's no sign yet of his body. It all seems to be going to plan.

I got the idea for Don's disappearance from my time living and working in Australia. A colleague once told me the story of the Aussie prime minister in the 1960s, Harold Holt, who simply disappeared into the sea one day. No one was quite sure if he had overestimated his swimming ability or committed suicide. In his case there was no note, so for Don that was a little creative variation of my own. Holt was never found, like many others who have simply disappeared into the water. But by misdirecting everyone to look for Don in the water it helped me to settle him into the woods.

***

'Any appointments today?' I call out to Justine as I eventually settle down at my office desk the next morning. I am already nursing my second cup of coffee of the day. I do have a nice office at the university and it relaxes me to look out of my window and see green spaces, the central quad and a conveniently placed oak tree that is home to several nesting birds. The vice-chancellor would have taken the tree down if he could, replacing it with an outdoor study hub. I'm glad the tree is protected – the hub idea sounds awful. Who plans an outdoor study hub in Lancashire – it rains 200 days of the year. Justine looks up at me over her half-moon glasses from across her connecting office.

'Just three meetings today,' she says, and I sigh. Pointless meetings are the bane of my working life. I should never utter anything useful or sensible in meetings as the prize for this seems to be an invitation to join another one. For a bunch of solitary sociopaths, academics do like a meeting, although usually just to posture and show off their intellects – I'm better than most at this. Justine comes through to see me with a bunch of papers in her hand.

'Some light pre-meeting reading for you,' she says, smiling as she drops a heavy bundle of papers in front of me.

'Jesus,' I say. She laughs.

'That's why you get paid the big bucks,' she says.

'Hardly,' I say. I earned far more money as a trader than I do now as an academic. Even if I do eventually make it to vice-chancellor, I will probably still only make £200,000. I had that as a bonus once in the city.

For the next thirty minutes she gives me a précis of the day ahead, placing priority documents in front of me for signing off as we speak.

'So, remind me who's up first?' I ask, swirling the remaining froth of my latte for a final gulp. As I glance at my computer screen, I see I already have over 100 new emails this morning and I try to remember why I wanted to be an academic.

'Whatever did we do before emails?' says Justine, catching my expression.

'Whatever indeed,' I say. Back in the day, I would never

have had 100 phone calls or letters and we always seemed to manage alright. Most of this communication must be superfluous information, and as I read through at pace, I conclude that indeed it is.

'Paul, Chris and Lee are coming here in fifteen minutes, then after that…' she says, while I groan. Paul and his team are from a problem area of staff that I inherited when I joined USL. The PVCs have cross-institute strategic responsibility for themes such as research, learning and teaching, enterprise, commercial estates, marketing and so on. But as academic PVCs we also manage the operational schools where all the student programmes are delivered. This morning's particular delegation of staff oversees our history programme that recruits almost no students. The vice-chancellor made it clear to me from the day he recruited me that he wanted that programme closed and those staff gone.

'Of course, vice-chancellor,' I had said. 'When would you like it done?'

'No rush Jez, give it a few months,' he told me. I found out later that several heads of school and PVCs had tried and failed to get rid of them over the years. But I do like a challenge. Paul in particular has been tying up USL with union interference, garnering sympathy from the wider academic community, and then levelling personal grievances and accusations of bullying at anyone making any progress. But, as I said, I do like a challenge and over the years my lack of empathy has served me well. It has meant I have an excellent track record of getting things done. I just need to work out which buttons to press to gain the biggest effect with people then I'll start pressing.

The history team's previous head of school hadn't lasted long, less than a year in fact before he moved on in frustration or was it after a breakdown, no one was quite sure. So I'm covering that portfolio too; it's a further task but it does keep me closer to the historians. I can more directly make their lives uncomfortable until they either leave voluntarily or until I can evoke sufficiently unprofessional responses from them to warrant sacking.

'Next up, after the history group, is your meeting with your heads of schools,' she says. There are nine heads of school across the university and four of them report to me. So, as I am covering for the humanities, I am both one of them and also their boss. It's a strange dynamic.

The heads of school are an interesting bunch but mostly alright. They are generally those staff who have leadership aspirations but are not quite there. This means they're probably destined to remain middle management for the rest of their careers, although they don't seem to realise this. Most have aspirations for my job but are not sufficiently 'complete' to ever do it. I, of course, am a complete psychopath.

Being a head of school is a thankless task, so I do have some respect for them. They spend almost all their time managing the sociopathic hordes of academics in their schools and have no time to develop their own careers. So, when a PVC role does eventually come up, they are deficient in some way or other through lack of opportunity to ever do anything other than crowd control. But the heads are generally affable enough to the PVCs in the hope of gaining our favour and possible sponsorship for a more senior role.

The one person I really despise at USL is my fellow PVC, Terry Peak. Peak is a short, fat, former dancer who masquerades as an academic and simultaneously as director of learning and teaching. He has the look of Toad of Toad Hall, but without the charm. He also oversees the liberal arts school which is failing spectacularly at attracting students. They score well on student satisfaction metrics, but if you have as many staff as you do students, then why wouldn't they all be happy. What a smug asshole he is. He works closely with the deputy vice-chancellor, who's the ultimate arbiter of student experience, and between them they enjoy telling everyone else how to teach, even though they have absolutely no talent for it themselves. But Peak is one of those sycophants who always seems to do alright because he says yes to every whim of the VC or DVC, however ridiculous it might be. He then delegates everything to his staff, so when it goes wrong, he blames them for it – I have to admire his strategy, it's the academic pyramid scheme. He's not nicknamed Teflon Terry for nothing, although I think Toad is more apt and better fits his physicality too. He's often seen wearing a green suit, waistcoat, and when in a heightened state of academic excitement has the very distracting habit of rubbing his thighs while simultaneously licking his lips. I often imagine him opening his mouth, flicking out a large tongue to grab an unsuspecting fly lingering too close in his vicinity.

My office attire is more straightforward, although well executed. I've heard people refer to me as the 'Designer Dean' and I don't mind that at all. Actually, I'm quite glad people notice, although I try to make style seem effortless. I'm usually to be found wearing a navy blue Hugo Boss suit, occasionally coupled with a smart tie, but ordinarily I favour an open neck, in a Thomas Pink or Ralph Lauren shirt. All this accessorised by my only jewellery – an Omega Speedmaster Moonwatch, the type worn by Neil Armstrong and Buzz Aldrin when they first landed on the moon. That was the year in which I was born, so it's always a convenient icebreaker conversation for anyone who has a keen eye for style, expensive watches and is happy talking about me. Although it's causing me considerable anxiety that I haven't been able to locate it since I buried Don.

The Tale of Being Neighbourly

Mid-afternoon on Christmas Eve in Cairns, Australia – it's hot as hell and Maxine's having her first chemotherapy treatment. I find it both upsetting and exciting at the same time. It's interesting to watch her voluntarily taking poison intravenously into her arm in the hope that it will make her better. It's fascinating really; voluntarily disabling her immune system to get better, meaning she will be susceptible to even the slightest bug that's floating around. Almost anything could kill her and I can't imagine what being that vulnerable must be like. It's so interesting to watch the patients in the ward, wondering which ones will make it. But she's being a good sport about it all now, having gotten over the shock. Thankfully she's stopped making too much of a fuss. I'm trying to disguise my interest and be supportive, which she seems to be appreciating. Her family too – they all think I'm great for looking after her. I'm not sure how I would respond if it were me, although I suspect I would probably just let myself die rather than be left vulnerable like this. It'd be more fun to quietly take myself off somewhere with a case of whisky and a whole bunch of drugs.

'Daddy, what's Jason doing?' asks Jamie when we arrive back home. I'm reversing the car into the garage and I take a look in the direction of Jason's house next door. He's sitting with a couple of his bogan mates and they already have a scattering of crushed beer cans at the feet of their deckchairs. It's Christmas Eve so it's forgivable today I suppose. They seem happy, joking about something.

'He's just sitting and having a drink with his friends,' I say.

'Why is he waving a finger at us?' asks Jamie. I look over to Jason again and this time I see he has his middle finger raised at us. His friends are giggling uncontrollably, nudging each other next to him. Maxine shoots me a look – she knows this will upset me.

'Get him Jez. For me,' she says and puts an arm on my shoulder. I've never seen her look like this. She looks translucent, close to death, but her eyes – those don't look dead. I see hatred instead. Is she really encouraging me to kill him? Surely not, but I feel myself get excited, changing before her like Bruce Banner into the Hulk. Uncontrollable anger is building in me, all directed and channelled towards Jason. There's no need for a theme song today; I'm just going to break his neck, right here and now. I put the handbrake on, turn off the engine, unclip my seat belt, open the door and stride from the car. 'Jez... get him,' whispers Maxine behind me. 'For me..' she says. Too right I'm going to get him.

I stride towards the group, scanning our connecting lawns, looking for something I can use to smash all of their frail bodies into pieces. Humans – so weak and ineffective. I'm glad I'm not one of them, a superior being altogether, and I'll show them my true self now. I'll take them all, but first Jason. I can't see anything obvious that I could use, so I just head straight for him with my fists clenched. The laughter stops but he's still sat in his deckchair, facing me with a smug expression and a beer can in his hand.

'Fuck off, Pom!' he shouts dismissively at me as I close in on him at speed. He's sitting down but as I close in, his expression is changing to one of worry. I can see it in his eyes. His friends are silent now, watching me to see what I will do. As I reach him, he starts to scramble to get up, but he stumbles from his chair and his foot catches its base making him tumble over, landing face down on his driveway with his chair on top.

His mates start laughing as he grapples around on the floor trying to untangle himself. Seeing him on the floor looking idiotic calms me and I feel the mist of hate slowly lift from my mind as I stand over him, beginning to laugh. As he recovers his composure, so do I. He gets to his feet to face me, angry-looking now or is it embarrassment? I think how pathetic he looks with his droopy moustache and pencil-thin biceps. Some beer has spilt onto his vest and he's trying to look nonchalant for his mates.

I have enough composure now to maintain a smile. I administer two stiff prods to the middle of his chest with my index finger. I speak and prod in rhythm, pausing after each word. 'DON'T BE RUDE,' I say loudly and slowly and I see him gulp. Before he can respond I turn and go back to the car.

'Jason is funny, Daddy,' says Jamie, back in the house. There are other words I could use to describe him, but I am relieved that was the extent of the incident. Maxine looks annoyed with me. Did she really mean for me to kill him? She saw me kill Tommy and that was for far less, but killing Jason in broad daylight would have been very unwise. Besides, it's my choice who I kill, my business, not hers. We won't speak of it again.

The Present Tale

'Come in,' I call out to the historians for my first meeting of the day. Justine's been keeping them at bay in her office until I'm ready for them. I like to keep them waiting for a few minutes longer than is strictly necessary to build their anticipation and emphasise the power dynamic for the meeting. As they come in, it amuses me to see how they make themselves at home in my office, as if they own the place. I have no idea why they want to see me this morning and I wonder exactly what issue it is that they will be outraged about today. As they enter, I see Paul is already red-faced, agitated and indignant about something, so here we go.

'How are we all?' I ask breezily as I move over to join them at the meeting table.

Paul doesn't respond or make eye contact with me. Why do so many people avoid eye contact? He's busy shuffling some papers he has brought with him. Chris seems happy to chatter nicely about the weather and Lee is laughing about something that Chris said, but which I can't see is even remotely funny. So, experience tells me Paul is here to engage in some serious business, Chris feels confident, measured, so will be the main support to Paul, while Lee is there to make up the numbers although he really doesn't feel comfortable being here at all, hence the giggling. So with that out of the way I'm already clear on the parameters for the meeting.

'We wanted to ask you about your decision not to enter us to the Research Excellence Framework,' says Paul. What I want to do is slap him around the face and say that's because you're not in any way excellent and neither's your research. But experience tells me that would not be the correct tone for the meeting.

'Oh yes?' I say, simply, instead.

'Yes,' says Paul. He is becoming redder and I notice a blood vessel pulsing in his neck just as it had for Leighton. 'Frankly, I am outraged,' he says and I almost giggle.

'Oh dear, I am sorry to hear of your outrage,' I say. This doesn't seem to help his mood. I now notice another blood vessel pulsing into prominence, this time on his temple. If it was on his leg, I would say it was varicose, given its erratic shape. He should get it looked at.

'We demand the decision is reversed immediately,' he says, pressing down hard on the papers he brought with him and now making eye contact. Lee is giggling more than ever; he must be nervous. I suspect he may have peed himself slightly. I can't help myself, so I wink at him and he carries on laughing. Paul does not laugh.

With coffee now in my belly, I feel reasonably invigorated and I wonder how far I can push Paul without it resulting in him launching a grievance against me with human resources. I imagine he's hoping to provoke *me* to do something imprudent in front of his witnesses, so it's a fine balance about how far to go. It's a ruse my predecessors often fell for. Once you go too far and a formal grievance process is launched by a member of staff or a team then it becomes virtually impossible to manage them. So I don't rise to Paul's bait. I relax, silently humming along to 'White

Horses', and think back fondly to what I was doing on Friday evening with Don.

'Oh, you demand, do you?' I say, eventually after I have hummed the first verse and chorus to myself. All three of the delegation are now looking at me intently, so I hope I was not singing out loud, although I suspect I may have swayed just a little with the chorus. It is a nice tune.

I sustain eye contact with Paul, doing my best not to blink in this battle of wills, much in the way Leighton used to exert authority over me. It seems to be having a similar effect on Paul and he blinks, then looks down to his papers again.

'Well, not *demanding* obviously, Jeremy, but really it is outrageous for us not to be entered…' he says, a little more defensively this time. He looks to Chris for support, who nods several times and enters the conversation at this point. I believe this was his cue to be the rational voice in the room after they hoped I would have taken the bait and engaged in a heated debate.

'Yes, I must say, a serious decision like this when taken with no consultation is very unreasonable and not in the best interests of the university,' says Chris, to which Paul nods vociferously and looks back towards me. Paul then shoots a look over to Lee as it seems it's his turn now. But he's still giggling, although trying to stop and make a contribution, which he seems unable to do. I let my gaze follow in his direction and my stare gets to him before he's even spoken, which I think unnerves him slightly so he just nods in support of his colleagues and carries on laughing. Chris shakes his head and tuts at him, before picking up the conversation himself.

'Yes, I fail to see how this is compliant with the university code of practice and we really feel it is a decision that should be reconsidered,' says Chris. They are all looking at me again now. This is where the group dynamic tries to apply peer pressure into reversing a decision. I expect it's worked very well for them on many occasions over the years, so you can't blame them for trying.

I've moved on to silently humming 'This Empty Place' by The Searchers, although not as a killing theme song. This one is just for fun, a soothing old song. I look thoughtfully towards the Kandinsky print I have on the wall behind Paul before replying.

'I appreciate this was not welcome news,' I say, to which they all nod. 'But, I am afraid the depth and breadth of your research simply does not meet the quality threshold for excellence I set for subject teams to be entered.'

Paul clears his throat and the blood vessel in his temple is pulsing again. 'But, but... How are you qualified to make that decision?' he says.

I'm sure I see his right hand clench into a soft fist. Maybe he would like to punch me or if he had a pen in his hand, could he be tempted to stab me? He looks like he has the urge to hurt me right now. I catch sight of Justine peering through the gap in the door we left ajar; she's quick to detect someone raising their voice.

'Look, Paul, quite simply you have only 200 citations of your research throughout the entirety of your career,' I say. He has a startled look on his face, surprised I had looked up his metrics. I look at the others who now appear equally surprised. 'Chris you have around 150 and Lee, well, you are yet to reach 100. So that simply means other researchers around the world just don't think you are important and are not engaging with your work.' I recline in my chair to watch how Paul will react to this. It's a measured, yet intentional evidence-based insult, so I'll see how it goes. I pay particular attention to Paul's facial colour and the increasing frequency of his pulsing blood vessels. After watching them for ten seconds I'd estimate his heart rate is at 150 beats a minute. This should make him breathless when he next speaks and if he stands up abruptly, he might even faint. I can't resist giving him another nudge.

'Of course, I am barely research-active myself these days, but my career citations are over 5000,' I say and as predicted, Paul is now gasping for breath and mopping his brow.

'This is just simply unaccept... ' he says, but can't finish.

'You see, what am I to do if no one is reading your work?' I say, honing in for the kill. I am at my most reasonable and it's me now looking to Lee for support, who actually nods back to me. 'My hands are tied, I am afraid Paul,' I say.

'But...' Paul is not giving up, but I am growing impatient now as I have other meetings, so I need to wrap it up.

'I'm happy to support you all with senior academic mentors to aid your development,' I add. Being near retirement age, this is clearly an insult too far for Paul, who stands up to leave, promptly experiencing a rapid change in blood pressure; he stumbles to hold on to the table. I see it coming and catch him.

'Steady on Paul, you need to be careful,' I say, supporting him so he doesn't fall.

'I'm alright,' he says gruffly and with that he leaves the room, supported by his colleagues.

'Paul was a bit shouty,' says Justine as we rearrange the room after they have left. She hands me the papers and agenda for the heads of school meeting.

'Yes, he did become a bit excitable,' I say. She laughs. It's time he retired, and with a few more gentle pushes here and there I think I can accelerate that process. It's been a successful start to the day.

I have a bit more time than I thought before the heads of school meeting. I check my phone and see I have a few new text messages. The first one is from Jamie asking how my journey was to Ormskirk last night. I text him back to let him know it was alright and tell him I will call this evening. I remember I need to check up how he's getting on at school too. He was having a problem with a bully a little while ago and I'm not sure that has fully worked itself out yet. He can be a sensitive lad.

I remember Jamie crying when Maxine was having chemotherapy in Australia and particularly when she lost her hair. I looked at the creases of his face while he cried for his mum. His whole face would contort, become bright red and his cheeks would be soaked in tears. Then he would grab me, fling his arms around my neck and ask me to make it all better.

The Present Tale

As I'm about to leave my office for the heads of school meeting, there's a knock on the door. It's annoying when people come to visit unexpectedly; invariably they want something. It's not like they come calling casually to see if the PVC is alright, or whether I fancy going for a coffee.

'Yes?' I call out, patting down the pockets in my jacket as I look around the room for my reading glasses.

'Hi Jez, just wondered if I could catch you for a moment?' It's Faye Martin and as momentary interruptions go, this one is OK. Faye is mid-thirties, blonde, cute and highly ambitious. She would be high on a sociopath scale too. She likes to tell me when she has had good press on a new research article, or anything else that shows she is in some way excellent. I suspect she would do anything that will help her career. I mean, anything.

'No problem, Faye,' I say and beckon for her to take a seat on the sofa that sits parallel to my desk. This position affords me a good angle to observe her cleavage, which is looking impressive enough today to warrant me delaying leaving for the meeting. I tend to use the sofa for softer, more informal visits – History Paul doesn't sit on my sofa. As she sits down, I think how she might look if I bent her over the meeting table. I struggle to shake this image from my mind as she tells me about a new study she is readying for submission to a journal.

'And so you see, Jez, I had no idea the journal would charge us a publication fee,' she says, which brings me back to reality and makes me more aware that I am now running late.

'Ah I see,' I say. How many times have I heard academics say this. Their casual indifference to money and assumption we'll pay for everything. There's always a story – they must think us stupid. She doesn't look embarrassed to be asking for money though.

'I'll think about it. Budgets are tight at the moment and I need to see how it fits our strategy,' I say.

'Oh, OK,' she says, sounding disappointed. She's very distracting, but it's best to stay away from work colleagues and especially subordinates. I did make an exception once and that was for Bella. But Bella had nothing obvious to gain from me; she was just someone I worked with.

Faye manoeuvres herself on the sofa before I can leave, leans over and positions the draft of her paper in front of me. Her cleavage is practically rubbing my cheek. One sudden movement of my head and I will have my face fully embedded between her breasts. She stays there for a moment longer than strictly necessary, turning the pages for me in silence. I'm not reading the article, I'm too distracted and she knows it, but she doesn't move.

I hear someone cough in the background as time stands still. I hear a throat being cleared again and sense Faye breaking the spell of the moment, turning away from me and towards the noise. This brings me back to reality. It's Justine, trying to attract my attention.

'Jez, your meeting is about to start,' she says, pointing to her watch. Faye retreats down to her original position back on the sofa, taking her breasts with her. I notice a look shared between the two women.

'Thanks Justine,' I say, and having tracked down my glasses I perch them on the top of my head as I gather my papers together. Faye gets up to leave at the same time.

'Can I book in to see you for a one-to-one soon?' she asks.

'Yes, sure. Justine will book something into the diary,' I say and she leaves the room ahead of me as I put my jacket on. Justine scribbles a note in her pad to arrange a convenient time.

'You need to watch that one,' she says. That's women's intuition for you.

'I know,' I say. 'It's under control.'

The Present Tale

At the heads of school meeting, The DVC is not there yet to chair it, but Terry Peak is unfortunately in the room already. I could hear his fake laughter down the corridor. He's telling a complex comedic tale to the respective heads of allied health and education who are both feigning smiles and intermittent laughter. I doubt what he is saying is funny but there is no accounting for taste. I make my way to the other end of the table away from the green-suited one.

I get on with reading the meeting papers, but I am soon distracted as I hear Peak reaching a crescendo in his tale. It makes my skin crawl to hear him and his fake laughter, mainly I suspect as I find it a very challenging technique to perfect myself. So I am a connoisseur of recognising fakeness with a fine ear. People do it to fit in to groups and show camaraderie, but the more I see it in others the more it irritates me. I could happily take his tablet computer and batter him with it. Thinking of this, I almost break out into a perfect fake laugh myself.

'Hi Jez,' says Derek as he sits down next to me. He's one of the less obvious narcissists in the group. The DVC enters the room and Peak lets out another particularly loud cackle of laughter to let everyone know just how popular he is. Derek looks at me and rolls his eyes. I smile at him, he's alright.

Two hours later and we are done. I was busy for most

of the meeting watching Peak and practising the Jedi mind skills I've recently seen in a *Star Wars* movie with Jamie. I spent twenty minutes of the meeting trying to crush his windpipe with the power of my mind and then when that failed, I attempted to use the force to make the ceiling strip lighting crash down, landing on his head. Neither proved effective strategies.

I recline back in my chair and stretch out as the meeting winds down and people move off to their next appointments. Between fantasising about killing Peak with lighting fixtures and generally being bored, I have almost no recollection of what was said in the meeting for the last ninety minutes or so. That's a worry – perhaps I have Alzheimer's disease?

'How is it going, Jez?' asks the DVC as I gather up my papers to leave along with the crowd. I never know what to think when asked that question. I shrug and pause at the door.

'Yes, all is OK, David, just busy you know,' I say. He nods in agreement as I start to leave, but he lingers.

'You seemed a bit distracted in there,' he says. I shrug – this is annoying. I hadn't thought anyone had noticed. I feel like saying he should try killing a vice-chancellor over his weekend and see how it affects his concentration on a Monday morning. I think if he knew what I'd been through, he could excuse me a bit of distraction. Also, I am more than a little concerned about just where I might have left my watch. Surely, I haven't left it with Don? It seems unlikely but I can't specifically remember whether or not I was wearing it when I buried him. Did I take it off to dig? I honestly can't remember.

'Oh really, distracted you say?' I ask.

'Have you heard about Don Chaucer?' he asks.

I'd rehearsed how to respond to this question a few times on my drive to Ormskirk on Sunday evening, but I have already used my feigned surprise response once when Bella called me. My mind drifts to Bella again and imagining her naked.

'Jeremy, are you OK?' David asks, mistaking my sexual distraction for grief. Annoyingly he puts his hand on my shoulder supportively. I hope I haven't inadvertently got an erection.

'Sorry. I was just thinking about Don and what could have happened to him,' I say.

He nods at me, but his hand is still there on my shoulder, rubbing now. He had better not hug me. I look down to my trousers and thankfully there is no sign of a hard-on.

'I thought that might have been upsetting for you,' he says. 'What with him being your former boss.' He shakes his head empathetically. 'Such a waste.'

'Yes, very sad,' I say, doing my best not to think of Bella.

'Yes, so sad, so talented,' he says, now patting me like a pet and I can't work out how to make him stop. Talented is going a bit far for Don. Old Chasey Chaucer got what was coming to him.

'Yes, very sad if he has taken his own life,' I say, trying to stoop down to drop my shoulders low so his hand breaks contact with me.

'Are you sure you should be here today?' he asks. I think about this, as I could do with some time to search for my watch, but I think that's not what he means.

'Oh I am alright, I'll soldier on,' I say.

'If there is anything we can do? I wasn't sure how close you were, but I see now he meant a lot to you.' This is interesting as I hadn't properly thought some people might offer me sympathy, assuming we'd been close.

'Yes we were quite close I suppose,' I say, shaking my head. He nods again and pats my shoulder a couple more times as we walk out of the room. Thankfully we avoid a hug.

★★★

Back at my desk I scroll through the news and see what is being said about Don, so I'm at least up to date. This is a much higher-profile kill than any other I have done in the past, even more so than Leighton and he became a local cause célèbre in Abingdon. Someone even called into the local radio station to dedicate a song to him. For such a small town it gave them a bit of excitement for a while. I must admit I am finding the news about Don a bit of a thrill now. But I hope this doesn't attract *so* much publicity that the authorities look too closely into it. Publicity is no friend to a serial killer; many a contemporary has become unstuck by too much media attention.

My mobile phone begins to vibrate in my pocket. It's Bella and I decide to answer it.

'Hey you. How's the day going?' she asks. She sounds excitable. I imagine her on top of me, kissing my neck.

'All fine here. It must be interesting where you are. What's the latest on Don?' I ask as nonchalantly as I can. The thought runs through my mind whether it's sensible to take calls from her at the moment bearing in mind I buried her boss in nearby woodlands.

'It's mayhem here, Jez. No one knows what's going on. There's an emergency board meeting this afternoon and it looks like Kate is taking over as acting VC,' she says.

'That sounds a good decision,' I say. Kate Rook has been the DVC at Drake's for a long time and is a safe pair of hands. She's not known for innovation, as you might expect for an accountant, but prudent management is no bad thing for a multi-million-pound business.

'Are you coming home next weekend?'

'Not sure, probably.'

I generally try to go home only fortnightly these days as it's useful for me to stay and get work done at USL. From time to time Bella also coordinates to come up and stay with me for the weekend. I do also like my own space, which this arrangement affords me. Maxine is not so keen on it, but Jamie is always busy so that seems to occupy her.

'Did you have something in mind?' I ask. I do feel I'm due some kind of reward for alleviating her of her lecherous boss. It's a shame I can't tell her about it.

'Oh I thought I might give you a nice surprise,' she says and I instantly feel excitement. She must be a mind reader.

'That sounds fun,' I say enthusiastically and look through my diary.

After I hang up, I realise that I do miss Drake's a bit, but obviously not Don. I close my eyes, hum 'White Horses' and think of his last moments. He couldn't decide whether to spend his final seconds grappling to rip the plastic bag from his head or to unpeel the parcel tape that was securing it in place beneath his chin. What a conundrum for him, but highly entertaining and vice-chancellors are supposed to be decisive, so it was a good test for him. I'd double bagged him anyway, so when he eventually decided to try the bag rather than the tape he immediately ran into trouble, realising too late there was another layer. In his last seconds I could see him give up, suck in the remaining air from the bag and accept his fate. It was then he trickled urine on to the carpet. It was just a small puddle.

The Tale of Being Neighbourly

The situation with Jason in Australia did not improve over the next few months. Then, one day as I mowed the front lawn, I looked over at him sitting in a deckchair, on his driveway, giggling again with his mates and drinking beer.

'You've missed a bit,' I hear him shout out, over the top of Midnight Oil playing from his stereo. Maybe a song of theirs could become his theme tune when I kill him. I really want to crush his windpipe in my hand and as I stop for a moment to mop my brow, I smile at him in a way that few people have seen. He smiles back and raises his beer can at me, while they are all giggling in chorus. What short memories they must have. 'Beds Are Burning' – could that be his song, I'm not sure. It's catchy but also a political track about the plight of indigenous people. It seems inappropriate; although I doubt bogan assholes like Jason have ever done anything positive for indigenous Australia. I'll leave it a while before I do anything to him as I want to avoid jail. Jamie would miss me if I were not around and in my view you can't dismiss the value of a good role model. So, I'll keep my hands off Jason and play nicely until the time I can pay him a visit when no one could ever link me to him. For now, at least his social gatherings are rarer after other neighbours spoke to him. Seeing Maxine with her bald head, clearly unwell during her chemotherapy, did at least get to them. But not him – he seems frustrated to drink alone more often now, just sitting with his music and boat. The empty beer cans I find in our pool most mornings are no doubt his. I see him drinking cans of XXXX beer and that's the brand I find in there. Tilting his can at me now is a provocation I think, but I won't bite. So I just smile and wave at him. As I turn back to mowing the lawn, I hear them laugh again.

Maxine will soon finish her chemotherapy treatments. Each time she has a round of it, she becomes totally helpless, vomiting into a bucket I hold up next to the bed for her. When she can finally eat, I try to get her to take soup that I feed to her with a spoon. It's exhausting running the household on my own so I hope she improves soon. I'm also taxi driver for Jamie, taking him wherever he needs to go, cleaner, cook and homework supremo. I've never been so tired, but at the same time I'm finding the logistical challenge of it all very interesting. Seeing how much I can take without breaking is a good test and I seem to be coping so far. Unfortunately, it's kept my hobbies on the backburner for a while and so I do feel a sense of frustration. There are times when I think Maxine might just quietly slip away and then once or twice, I think placing a pillow over her face would be a kindness. I never do it of course.

When Maxine gets better, we move back to the UK for me to take up a new post at Francis Drake's University in Carlisle. It's not a strong university but it'll be my first chair, so I don't really care. I will have to decide if I can get to Jason before we leave. Moving country could be a good time to take care of business, just as I did with Leighton.

The Present Tale

Friday morning and I'm excited it's the end of the week as I'll go home today. I gather up my laundry in the flat, ready to bring home for Maxine, and idly think about what fun I am going to get up to with Bella later in the day too. I have a couple of appointments before I finish off at work just after lunch with a one-to-one with the DVC. I expect he wants to check my welfare again.

There's still no sign of my watch and Maxine tells me she has had a thorough search for it at home. I've turned the flat inside out too. I think Maxine could tell I was stressed about its whereabouts as she started to ask more questions. She sounded tense, which is never a good sign.

When I arrive at my office, I turn on the computer and wait for it to start. I close my eyes and dream of Bella and what we'll being doing later today.

'Where were you just now?' asks Justine, standing next to me when I open my eyes.

'What do you mean?' Justine glances down at my crotch and then back up again at my face. As I look down, I see I am erect.

'Ah,' I say and cross my legs. Fortunately, she laughs; I imagine she will have seen plenty of erect penises in her time, although looking at her, not for a while. She's a smoker I think, or maybe a former smoker. You can tell from the yellowish colour of her teeth, one of which is gold-plated. Her skin has that aged look about it that some women get when they have been too keen to get out in the sun. Bella is not much younger than Justine but has that classical European look of sophistication that British women yearn for but never quite achieve. Justine tells me about the remaining reports I need to complete before leaving. As she transcribes some notes to her pad, I watch the angle of her hand rhythmically undulating on the page as she writes. It makes me think of Bella again and I drift away.

'Gone again?' asks Justine. She's laughing and I see her looking at my crotch. Is she coming on to me – I hope not. I ignore her this time and turn slightly away as I re-cross my legs. It was funny the first time, now it's just creepy.

The Tale of Being Neighbourly

After moving back to the UK, we have a considerable period of peace and quiet. Maxine's relatives visit us, we visit them, Jamie has started school in Carlisle and Maxine is happy to be closer to family support networks. She's stronger too, recovering from chemotherapy, and after a few months, close to her usual self. I even see her reflection occasionally in shop windows behind me from time to time, so I know she's started following me again. It means I need to be more careful in my movements with Bella and ensure Maxine is busy with Jamie's schedule as much as possible.

I had of course fantasised about killing Jason before we moved back to the UK, but I'd been too busy looking after Maxine to indulge that, so, reluctantly, I let it pass. At that time, I could also have been a suspect if anything happened to him, given that our animosity was well known. I'd considered torching his beloved boat when leaving the country as a parting gesture but that just seemed petulant. He would also have marine insurance, maybe even welcoming it as a means to get a new one. So, I fought back the desire to deal with him in an unsatisfactory way and waited for an opportunity to play the long game.

My father died while we were in Australia, a lifetime of drinking and chain-smoking eventually catching up with him. I found it ironic that one of my lasting childhood memories of Dad was trying to sing live Elvis for him. He died just like the King too, trying to defecate forcefully on the loo and having a heart attack. It's not glamorous to die with poop hanging from your backside but at least he was in good company.

Some of my relatives have been in touch, but thankfully my sister and her new husband Glen have not. They managed to clear Dad's bank accounts, sold his possessions, and are now newly based somewhere else in the UK. It was frankly a relief and my gift to our parents is to not to exact any revenge upon them for ripping me off. However, Jason – my bogan neighbour – does not have the benefit of being a blood relative. I continue to feel an increasingly strong desire to properly deal with him although the problem is finding the right opportunity.

As time back in the UK passed, for many months, then a year and beyond, I worried Jason might die. I longed for him to die of course, but by my hand and not some natural cause. If that happened, I would feel totally robbed and as time went on, I began to fear I might never get to him at all. Until one day, two years after returning to the UK, an opportunity arose for me to take a short academic trip to the University of Queensland in Brisbane.

Brisbane is in the same state as Cairns, but Queensland is enormous. So being in the same state doesn't mean much much as there's approximately 1700 kilometres between the two cities. It's not so far if you fly, that only takes two hours or so – by car it would be a twenty-plus-hour journey. But I readily agreed to the opportunity for a visit to Brisbane although really I could have accomplished all I needed via video conferencing. Nevertheless, it was an opportunity to collaborate with my old Aussie colleague Lachlan and to stay with him and his wife Kamila, with whom we had become close as a couple over the years. My trip was tied to the dates of the research grant we were applying for and so it would still require an element of luck to get to Jason, but it was the best chance I'd have if I could just get to Cairns.

Over the next couple of weeks, I excitedly plan my trip to Australia. Maxine and Jamie are disappointed not to be joining me, although they understand it is just a brief work visit. Going by road seemed the best way to get to Cairns undetected and I will have to carry out this element of my visit in total secrecy. I'll need to acquire a car that can't be traced for the drive and I will need some luck that he'll be in town. But the unpredictability does make it exciting.

Finally my plans are in place; I'm due to visit Brisbane for three days, then after that I'll take a further three days' holiday on the Sunshine Coast, just up the road, for some private rest and relaxation. Maxine even agreed it would be good for me to have three days there for some swimming in the sea and relaxing at the beach before heading home. Only that is not what I will be doing; instead I'll be making a neighbourly visit to Cairns.

The Tale of Being Neighbourly

I arrive in Brisbane, a full two years after moving back to
the UK. It feels strange being back, as though no time has
passed and the world has stood still. I've been to Brisbane
airport many times; the coffee bars and food outlets look
just as I remembered them and the weather is perfect.
No seasonal readjustment is needed as July is the height
of the British summer and yet it is also the middle of the
Queensland winter. So, basically, they are well matched for
acclimatisation – both seasons warm enough to wear shorts
and a T-shirt, and yet not so warm as to be in scorching
heat and humidity.

I have a plan about how to get to Cairns but there are
still so many unknown variables, principally about Jason's
movements. I've obviously not been there to keep an eye
on him and it'll be down to luck whether I can track him
down. I don't spend too much time on the plane agonising
about this, deciding it's better to get loaded on miniature
whisky bottles instead. This makes the cabin crew look
more alluring than ever, although I am disappointed none
of them summon me into a cubicle to fulfil their mile-high
ambitions. I imagine they have all done this already; it's
probably part of their initiation process.

After landing, I wait for my luggage at the airport and
hear a familiar Eastern European accent from behind me.

'Jez darling,' says Kamila, grabbing me in a big bear-hug. I can feel the softness of her large breasts as she clings tightly to me and I try not to let my cabin crew frustrations turn into a fully fledged erection. I quickly pull clear of her embrace in case she can feel the first signs of stiffening which is happening faster than I can readily control.

Although now in her late thirties, Kamila is still a very attractive woman. She's stereotypically Czech – blonde, tall and inordinately heavily breasted for a slim woman.

'Good to see you, Kamila,' I say, standing back a metre from her as I try to regain control of my crotch. 'You look good,' I say, not sure if it's the excess whisky in my system, hours spent visualising cabin crew in various acts, or genuinely as I had misremembered her. Whatever way, she really does look stunning. I look around her in the arrivals hall to see if I can see Lachlan anywhere.

'He's waiting in the car,' she says, noticing me scanning the room. She kisses me on the lips and this time slips her tongue gently into my mouth, which means I feel a rush of blood again. 'I've missed you,' she says. This might be more awkward than I thought as her husband is a good friend. Then there is of course beloved Bella too. Pure, virtuous, angst-ridden and downright filthy Bella. Bella who is not here and will never know if I sleep with Kamila.

I did have sex with Kamila one time while we all lived in Australia, but I don't think she can have told Lachlan about it or else he would have mentioned it for sure. He's a good guy, but that is unlikely to extend to sharing his wife.

We walk through the arrivals lounge together and my attention has definitely shifted from cabin crew to Kamila now. It wasn't particularly memorable sex we had that one time, but I don't think it was wholly bad either. She could be worth another go – I shall have to try and remember the details of it more vividly later before I decide. She just needed some attention back then as Lachlan is always very focused on his work.

'So how have you been?' I ask her and hand over the duty-free bag I'm carrying with a bottle of gin in it. She takes the bag, kisses me on the cheek this time and locks arms with me to walk me out of the terminal.

'I'm fabulous, sweetie, thank you for asking,' she says and continues to talk non-stop for the next five minutes until we reach the car. I zone out from what she says before we even get to the car. I think this was perhaps why I wasn't too bothered about her; she's a bit dull.

I can see Lachlan sitting in the driver's seat, typing something into his phone. This is exactly as I remember him, still addicted to emails and messaging. He had a gay lover back in the day, but I'm not sure Kamila ever knew about it. He told me about it once, a Nigerian visiting academic. He'd seemed quite excited about it all and for Lachlan, who is the most laid back of Aussies, surprisingly animated.

'Hey Lachy,' I say, depositing my case in the trunk with a heavy lift. He could have gotten out of the car to give me a hand, but he doesn't. I close the trunk and settle into the front passenger seat next to him in his new Toyota SUV. He grunts something inaudible to me and finishes off a message.

'Lachlan!' says Kamila, in a shrill voice from the back seat and slapping him on the shoulder. 'You've not seen Jez in ages, get off that phone!' It's good to see they haven't changed. That's the nice thing about old friends, no false niceties just straight back into normality.

'Sorry Jez, mate, one sec and I'll be right with you,' he says as he evidently has moved on to responding to another pressing message. He hits send and then looks up for the first time. 'Right, where were we?'

'You might have given me a hand with my case you lazy sod,' I say. Kamila gives him another slap, but he and I share a look this time and laugh. It's good to see him.

Kamila continues to talk non-stop from the back seat but is thankfully drowned out when Lachlan turns on the radio to catch up on some of the latest tennis news. She talks even louder in response and I watch him itching to increase the volume of the radio further as she raises her voice. He decides not to, as her noise blends into the background.

'Still playing then?' I ask.

'Mmm, sorry?' says Lachlan.

'Tennis. Still playing tennis?' I say.

'Ah. Yes indeed, let me tell you...' he starts to say. Lachlan always comes to life when you show interest in his hobby. So now both of them are competitively chatting away on parallel topics. I settle into my chair and snuggle down without really listening to either of them. I don't think they need me to participate anyway. I rest my head and close my eyes, listening to the background noise. That was such a long flight without any sleep.

It's a forty-five-minute drive to their house in Brisbane and the next thing I know, we are pulling into their garage. I'm not sure they noticed I was asleep as they are still chatting, but not to each other. Rubbing my eyes, I stagger into their house hoping they will just direct me to a bed.

'Gin and tonic darling?' Kamila shouts to me as I put my case down in their hallway. She's already heading off to the kitchen to make it before I can answer. I imagine this means Lachlan is still teetotal; I know she doesn't like to drink alone. As a teetotaller, he doesn't approve of her drinking – I can understand that though, I have seen it exaggerate her mood. As a passionate type, it can lead her to some poor decisions, like the one she made with me. I watch her backside sway into the distance, which wakes me up slightly.

I settle down on a comfy sofa in the living room with Lachlan and watch him search through the sports channels while I wait for my gin and tonic. Through the patio doors I can see their pool lights are still on. I miss having a pool – such a contrast to grey old England.

Lachlan has found a football match on TV and simultaneously moved on to his tablet device to pull up some documents. 'So, Jez, what do you think about the grant proposal?' he asks as Kamila reappears and hands me my drink. She's made herself one too and I see Lachlan give her a disapproving stare. She shrugs at him and takes a sip.

I groan at the thought of looking at the grant proposal and then realise I did this out loud. To which Kamila laughs and Lachlan looks embarrassed. It is the reason I am here, but right now I'd prefer to take a sip of my drink, recline into the softness of the sofa and maybe nap a bit.

'Lachy… Can we chat about it in the morning?' I say.

'Lachlan! Don't bother him with that now you idiot,' says Kamila and she slaps his leg as she settles down next to him.

'Ah OK, sorry,' he says. He closes his tablet and starts to chat engagingly with the both of us for the first time. For the next hour we share stories of when we used to hang out together, reminiscing over old times. They had been good friends for a long time and were supportive when Maxine became ill. None of our UK relatives visited us over that tricky time and so Lachlan and Kamila almost became our Australian family, a valuable local support network even if that was a two-hour flight away. I lose track of how many times they popped up to see us.

It was on one of those trips to support Maxine that Kamila also offered to support me. Lachlan had stayed in Brisbane that time, and she and I had both been drinking heavily one night when Maxine had gone to bed. I was surprised but it'd also been such a long time since I'd had sex that it was nice to be close with someone, anyone really, although I didn't tell her that. I'd always liked her and even if she was a bit dull, she was also kind and attentive. I had also long been fascinated by the shape of her breasts and on more than a few occasions, I had often idly wondered what they looked like naked.

It had been a nice distraction from Maxine's chemotherapy and was an opportunity for me to indulge in something selfish at a time when I was acting as a primary carer. So, when she lay down and told me to just use her, I had gratefully taken advantage of the situation and readily did so. It must have been for a good hour or so and afterwards we were both sweating heavily. I know I was exhausted and with Maxine asleep in the next room it was certainly exciting. It was fine as a one-time thing but looking back she was no Bella. After Kamila heard I got the job at Drake's she became more distant too and barely visited in the last few months. In fact, I am not sure she visited us at all.

The Present Tale

My last task of the day before I can finally leave work and drive to my rendezvous with Bella is to have my one-to-one meeting with the DVC. I am hoping this is not just more sympathetic talk of Don Chaucer and that he doesn't waffle on for too long. He can be a bit old and slow – I have to refrain myself from finishing his sentences sometimes.

'Come in Jeremy,' says David as I knock on his door.

I take in the surroundings of his office – it's much bigger than mine, so I have some office envy. It's a bit ugly though – he lacks taste and I'm not sure what it is he's done to earn such a room. Its aspect is not much better than mine, I know I can see nestling birds in the oak tree from my office window while he just has a view of the nasty 1960s fountain at the edge of the quad. The fountain always looks like it needs a good clean and the central figure looks like a slave with water dripping from a small penis. It's badly designed, so depending on the angle, it could also be a mermaid with a chain around her neck, squirting water from a protruding belly button. The only certain thing about it is that it was the result of a far too facilitative student project back in the day.

I look around the room, evaluating its size in my head. From a quick estimate I think the office is at least five square metres bigger than my own. I would be good at the job too, certainly better than this old ditherer. I look at him, sniff the air and can smell the scent of death on him. Cats are very good at sniffing it out too apparently – it's a musty odour and he reeks of it. Perhaps I should be proactive and hasten the process. It would be very easy – I could just pick up his frail body and throw him out of the window. The fall would surely kill him and if I aimed properly, I could ensure he also took out the awful fountain. Then when the VC invites me to take his post, I wouldn't even have that annoying edifice as a view from the window. Alternatively, would anyone notice if I took one of his immaculate pencils placed on his desk and drove it up his nostril into his brain? I'm now fixated on how far the pencil could reach if I pushed it hard. I estimate it would reach well behind his eyeballs, assuming it didn't break.

'Hi David, how's it going?' I ask, settling myself down onto his sofa. I convey a casual, friendly demeanour and do my best to stop looking at his pencils. I'm in a hurry to get back to sweet Bella and so I need to focus.

'Good Jeremy, really good actually,' he says, looking pleased with himself. No one should look that happy. If I did kill him, I would get a substantial uplift in my salary too. I look back at the pencils on his desk – it would be too messy, I think.

'Oh yes?' I say.

'Yes, Jeremy. I have some news I wanted to share with you,' he says. What does he have to say that is of more interest than the thought of skewering his brain with a pencil?

'What is it, David?' I ask, giving him the benefit of the doubt.

'It's a funny story actually…' he says, launching into a monologue. Jesus, old people. I'm in a hurry.

'I don't mean to rush David, but…' I say.

'Oh yes, of course, my dear boy,' he says. 'I wanted you to know that I am retiring.'

'Oh, I see,' I say, and this is indeed interesting, enough to gain my full attention and make me relax into my seat. I can spare a few minutes for him.

'Yes, the vice-chancellor and I have agreed the terms of my departure and you see, our plans concern you.' I feel warm and fuzzy, vindicated for all my hard work and embarrassed I was fantasising about killing a respected colleague with one of his pencils. What a dear man he is. Bella can wait for bit. Does he have some champagne, I wonder?

'That's great David, you will be very much missed and I would be delighted… ' I say, interrupting the old windbag. But he interrupts me.

'As I was saying, it concerns you… and also Terry, in fact,' he says. My heart sinks as I think of Terry Peak. How is that fat ineffectual dancer even mentioned in the same breath as me. My thoughts turn to skewering Peak's brain with a pencil now.

'Terry and I, how so?' I ask, dreading the answer. I know Peak has done his best to ingratiate himself with both the VC and DVC but surely they must have noticed he wears a green suit?

'Would you like a coffee, I've got this new machine…?' asks David, raising himself from his seat and moving with surprisingly good pace for a man in his sixties. I can already see it's one of those naff coffee pod devices, but he is already upon it before I can call him off. These machines were all the rage five years ago, but they never make a decent coffee, just a lukewarm, weak coffee solution. I bet he has one of those that use powdered milk too.

'That would be lovely,' I say.

'Have I shown you my new coffee machine?' he asks.

I shake my head enthusiastically. 'No, I don't think so. Is it any good?' I ask. He drones on with a detailed explanation of how it works for an eternity and as I look at my wrist for my missing watch, I know Bella will be worried where I am if I don't leave soon.

'I managed to reclaim it as an expense actually from one of our widening participation grants,' he says, looking rather pleased with himself.

'Great,' I say. 'Useful you could use the grant like that.' The Office for Students would take a dim view of using a Learning and Teaching grant aimed at increasing minority participation to buy a coffee machine. I should report him.

'It could be yours soon,' he says, patting it gently as it steams into action.

'Super,' I say. It will be the first thing in the bin when I take the job. I look around the room – this will need redecoration too. We sit sipping tepid, weak Americanos in his office. I can barely keep it down.

'Nice,' I say, breaking the silence. He nods at me, closing his eyes to savour the smell of the coffee. Just look at him – he deserves to die, and quickly.

'So, Jeremy,' he says. 'You want my job, do you?'

I laugh gently, doing my best to appear ambivalent to it, so I shrug.

'It would obviously be an honour, David, if you think

I am the right candidate, but obviously I have not been seeking this and I am also happy in my current position.' If I don't get it, I will either wipe out all those in my way or simply move elsewhere. One thing is for certain, I will not be passed over for Terry Peak.

'What were you saying about Terry?' I ask casually.

'Ah yes. You realise being DVC is largely a Learning and Teaching role?' he says.

Of course I realise this, I spend most of my working life interpreting and operationalising the ridiculous and impractical Learning and Teaching policies that flow from his bloody office. You would like to think people committed to Learning and Teaching were the best teachers, but this really is a perversity of higher education. That portfolio seems to attract the weaker-minded academics like a magnet drawn to an easy life. It's also like they create their own language of absurd, yet vast acronyms and pseudo-intellectual terminologies that we all have to learn before they change their mind, just to keep us guessing. I once sat through a two-hour debate on whether their department should be Teaching and Learning, or Learning and Teaching. For now it is Learning and Teaching but I forget why.

'Of course, I realise that David, and as you know, I am a real champion of your Learning and Teaching initiatives,' I say.

'Hmmm,' he says and deliberates for a moment as he sips his coffee. I have abandoned further attempts to drink mine and left it to decompose on his occasional table.

'I do see your potential Jeremy, and genuinely believe you have the capabilities to be a great DVC,' he says, and

I nod sagely back at him in agreement. 'But are you sure this is your priority?' he asks. It's a good question and of course it is not, as I will spend the first six months undoing his work, sacking Peak and the rest of the Learning and Teaching troupe. I shall make the university the beacon of research it was meant to be. However, promotion is promotion and this will leave me only one step away from the ultimate prize of being a vice-chancellor.

I look him meaningfully in the eyes. 'David, it is absolutely my passion and I will do my utmost to continue your excellent work,' I say. He pauses again and now even puts down his coffee, which is not a good sign.

'It is just… I hear things from Terry, and as you could probably imagine he is in the running for this position too,' he says, looking at me intently. My dislike for Peak is palpable now – this could be a major setback.

'Oh really – what do you hear?' I ask, my knuckles turning white.

'He says you often belittle the achievements of the Learning and Teaching team,' says David.

'Really?' I ask. What a shit.

'And you should know, he is firmly a Learning and Teaching man,' he says. Of course he is.

I reassure David of my commitment to the role and he changes the subject on to more social matters, but I see he's watching me so I decide to revisit the coffee.

'Delicious,' I say as I force down another mouthful.

I make a move to leave as I am now so late for Bella. 'One other thing, regarding you and Terry,' he says before I fully raise myself from the sofa.

'Oh yes?' I ask.

'The vice-chancellor has decided to take my recommendation on which of you should take over as DVC.'

I sink back down. Despite being handicapped by both his appearance and his lack of ability, Peak has clearly done enough to get himself well and truly in the game, probably even ahead.

'I see. When do you expect to make this recommendation?' I ask. He clasps his hands together in front of his face in a sombre, prayer-like position.

'I anticipate coming to a conclusion towards the end of next week. Probably Thursday and certainly no later than Friday,' he says. I nod and thank him for the dreadful coffee. Outside his door I jab a swift kick at his confidential waste bin and manage to dent it, which makes me feel moderately better. I visualise feeding Peak into a shredding machine but see the impracticalities; however, if he wants some competition for the DVC role he has found it. My mind wanders back to Tommy from my student days – a pleasant enough lad. He was a bit cocky, had a regional accent, bad teeth and was in my way. Peak is in my way, just like Tommy, so game on.

The Tale of Being Neighbourly

Kamila is still talking on the sofa and has now topped up her gin and tonic three times. Mine is barely touched and I keep drifting in and out of consciousness.

'How is Maxine darling? You must tell us how Maxine is.'

'Oh, she's well. She's working again,' I say. Maxine has stayed in banking through the years and it was always easy enough for her to pick up a job when we moved. When she recovered from cancer, she wanted to get back out to work.

'Do you need to call her, Jez? You have called her, Jez, to let her know you are here safely?' Kamila looks worried.

'No not yet, I'll call when I go to bed.'

'You must call her, Jez, she worries so and will think badly of me as a hostess if you don't call. Tell me you will call her!'

'I'll call.'

'Right – time for bed young man!' says Kamila, snatching my glass and leading me off by the hand. 'Say goodnight to him, Lachlan!' she shouts as we leave the room. Lachlan grunts, looks up from his tablet screen momentarily and waves a hand in my direction.

'This looks great, Kamila,' I say as she shows me to the freshly made bed in their guest room. She turns up the speed of the ceiling fan, which gives the room a cooling breeze.

'I bet you aren't used to warm nights anymore?' she says. That's true, I feel sweaty despite the action of the fan and wish they had the air conditioning turned on. I'll fire it up when she leaves the room.

'Maxine really was OK with you staying here, Jez?' She asks.

'Of course, why wouldn't she be?'

'Oh, you know, after our thing. She warned me off you.'

'Ah, I didn't know that.'

'Yes, it was a bit scary actually, the things she said she would do.'

'So that's why you stopped visiting?'

Kamila nods and dabs her eye, before grabbing me for another bear hug.

'It's so great you are here, Jez; we've missed you terribly.'

If truth be told, Maxine was not at all happy I was staying with them and so when I said I would be taking three days alone at the Sunshine Coast she did seem more positive. I just thought it was her usual possessiveness that meant she didn't want me to stay with them. It makes sense now.

'Thanks, Kamila. See you in the morning,' I say.

The next thing I know, it's 8 a.m. My T-shirt is soaking wet with sweat – I didn't make it as far as the air conditioning, nor to call Maxine. When I wake, I see a bunch of missed calls and messages from her, so I dial her number. She sounds angry and asks me a lot of questions. After I placate her and manage to hang up, I see some messages from Bella too, wishing me a safe trip and so I call her as well. Predictably it turns sexy.

The next two days go well. Kamila takes me to a bunch of sightseeing locations around Brisbane in the mornings; in the afternoons I work on the grant application with Lachlan and in the evenings we all visit nice restaurants and even a few cocktail bars.

By the third day of my visit, we have made such good progress with our application that it looks like we can make a very optimistic bid to the Economic and Social Research Council for a project looking at financial inequalities across developed nations.

'You could stay with us for three more days, Jez. I can't understand why you would want to go to the Sunshine Coast!' says Kamila as I pack my clothes.

'Oh, I don't want to be any bother,' I say. I have a busy and exciting schedule ahead of me for the next three days. Besides, Maxine has been getting very edgy about me being here and I did overhear her having a tense call with Kamila last night. It would be better all-round if I left today. I guess Kamila is just being polite, she must feel awkward about Maxine. Other than her usual tactile touches and flamboyance, there has been no further hint of anything sexual from her, so I imagine she has been scared off. Although in some ways I'm relieved as I do want to try to be good for Bella.

***

My drive to the Sunshine Coast only takes an hour on the main highway. In this part of the world satnav systems are largely irrelevant – you really can't miss the correct direction as there are limited options. I park the hire car in a highly visible spot in the motel car park, check-in, scatter some clothes around the room and then head directly to the beach for a peaceful walk along the waterfront. It'll be dark in a few hours and it's then that I need to leave on my long journey to Cairns. Right now, my peaceful stroll in the lapping waves is also a reconnaissance mission to see if I can spy any reasonable locations to steal a car. The hire car I used to get here could be instantly traced to me and if it stays in the car park it would certainly help my alibi. With any luck I will be up to Cairns and back within forty-eight hours and never missed.

The Sunshine Coast is a sleepy seaside resort, more of a locals' getaway than the Vegas of Australia down the road at the Gold Coast. But there are still plenty of people around. Strolling along the beach I think how nice it is, feeling sand under my feet, occasionally covering them with clear, cool water. Perhaps it was a mistake moving back to the UK from Australia, but it had been a decent career opportunity at the time. As I look up to my left above the sandbanks, I can see a few scattered hotels and a couple of open air car parks with views out over the waterfront. When I turn around and return to the motel, I will take a path closer to the car parks and properly check those out.

By 7 p.m. I am back in my motel room. It's now dark and I'm having a lie-down, relaxing before leaving, having completed a full check of car parks along the promenade. I am skilled enough to hotwire a car, but I am not good at doing it quickly. I was almost caught doing this once and so I'm hoping some hapless Aussie will have been kind enough to have left a car unlocked with the keys in it for me. For some reason many Aussies seem to think it's a good idea to leave their keys tucked in the sun visor – it's like an invitation to take them.

There's a knock on my motel room door which startles me. I stay silent, lying motionless on the double bed. Perhaps the knock is on one of the rooms either side of me. Sound carries when rooms are packed tightly together and the walls seem pretty thin. I stay still, waiting to see if I hear anything further; it can't be someone for me, unless it's housekeeping, I guess. I hear another knock, this time it's a fast, repeating knock, so I decide to see who it is. I have images of police at my door, but surely not; I haven't even done anything yet.

I ease myself off the bed and gently edge towards the door. Whoever it is will be able to see the light is on, so there is no point pretending I'm not here. There is no peephole in the door, which is unhandy, so I unlatch it, not sure what to expect. Opening it confidently, I see a familiar face – Kamila.

'Hello, darling!' she says as I open the door. I stand in the open doorway to block her entry. This is an unexpected turn; what does she want? She reaches forward and gives me one of her bear-hug greetings.

'Aren't you going to let me in then, sweetie?' she says, squeezing my crotch. Oh dear, it had all been going so well.

'Oh, OK. Sure,' I say, scrambling to work out what to do.

Kamila releases me and pushes on into the room. She is full of bustle and chatter as usual. She has a bottle of something fizzy in her hand, but I can't drink too much as I have a long drive ahead of me.

'This is a bit unexpected,' I say to her.

'Yes, darling, but your visit is so brief and I wanted to say goodbye properly,' she says. I notice she's wearing stockings under her tight skirt and I start to feel aroused. I take a look at my watch, trying to work out possible timings for an amended schedule. I look at her again and now see her silk vest top is clinging tightly to her breasts. I can't see the brand but it looks expensive and mauve is a colour that suits her. I wonder what the top would look like wet. It looks familiar too – she's worn it before I think, but I can't place where.

'Do you remember this outfit, Jez?' she asks.

'Umm. Not really,' I say as she closes up to me, pulling me towards to her. She looks disappointed and motions as if to leave, but then just as suddenly, she is upon me again smiling and laughing.

'You are terrible, Jez, but I love you anyway. I wore it in Cairns.'

'Ah yes, I remember now,' I say.

'I can't stay long. Lachlan will be back from the tennis club soon,' she says before she forcefully plunges her tongue in to my mouth. It's warm and she flicks it violently, meaning I feel social pressure to wiggle mine back. When I do, she groans in pleasure, and then holds my head, taking charge. I remember what it was like the last time we had sex – hard, sweaty and a lot of fun. I've probably got an hour or so.

***

Two hours later and I start walking at pace towards the car park next along to my motel on the promenade, cursing that I hadn't made more thorough plans about already getting a stolen car already in place. I'm feeling physically exhausted and a little sore from our exertions.

There's a bar next to the first car park; it looks like a sports bar and I peer through the door, seeing there's a match on inside. It looks like an AFL game – a sport I've never quite got to grips with. The Aussies love it and so they should be well entertained for the evening until it finishes. I subtly try a few car door handles as I drift along the first row, trying not to look suspicious, but they're all locked. Curse the Australian criminal DNA, they must assume everyone else is crooked.

'Any change, mate?'

'Excuse me?' I say and look down and see a homeless guy sitting on the Tarmac with his dog. He has a upturned baseball cap lying next to him with a few coins in it, but I've been wary of beggars for a long time – ever since Daniel.

'Some change, mate, you have any?' he repeats and holds out a hand. I do have some change but I'm not sure I want to share it, then I spy he has a mobile phone next to him. I could do with a non-traceable phone for the next couple of days.

'How much for your phone?' I ask.

'Not for sale, mate,' he says.

'I'll give you fifty dollars,' I say. He shrugs and hands me the phone, so I give him the money.

A group of people pass by along the promenade, and I'm acutely conscious this is a public place, so I make myself look a bit less suspicious by checking my watch as if I am waiting for someone to exit the bar. I'm relieved they continue on their way, but I decide it isn't ideal to hang out here too long.

This car park seems a dead loss for accessible cars although the phone will be handy. Even if I manage to steal a car, I'm dreading the thought of the twenty-hour drive ahead. I have to adjust my crotch a couple of times too – I might have overdone it with Kamila, which could be uncomfortable on the journey.

I give up on the car park and for a moment think of risking it and taking the hire car after all, but that would be the lazy approach. Now walking briskly along the promenade, I pass a Jeep SUV parked on the roadside and have a stroke of luck, noticing its keys dangling in the ignition. This looks too good to be true, but I take a subtle look around me and can't see anyone else in close proximity, so I open the door and jump in. I turn the key in the ignition and the engine starts up first time, purring into life. I press my foot down on the accelerator put some music on the stereo system and head for Cairns imagining slicing Jason's limbs off with a samurai sword, although a baseball bat will do just as well. I'll pick one up on the way.

The Present Tale

After escaping from the DVC, I'm finally free of commitments for the day and gleefully walk to the car park. Irritatingly I am now preoccupied with Terry Peak rather than Bella, which is a mood killer. What must he have said to David Lees about me? I do admire his self-interest and opportunism, but he has to realise there will be consequences. It'll take some creative thinking if I'm to get rid of Peak before Lees takes a decision on the DVC role next week.

I could try to discredit him but that could take months or years so I rule that out as being impractical. Perhaps I should just kill him, and indeed that would be the most enjoyable solution, but with almost no planning time it could go badly wrong and I still have loose ends with Don. It's a bit too much to have all this on my plate right now.

I only killed Don so swiftly because he was pestering Bella. She's the one thing keeping me sane and I think I might actually need her. This is the first time I've ever truly felt I could need someone else and I don't like that much. It makes me feel very vulnerable. But perhaps it could be a good thing? I could make a fresh start with her and maybe I might even ask her to leave her husband so we could settle down. Maybe I don't need the promotion to DVC at all – I could give up my hobby and marry Bella instead. It's me she loves and not her husband. Maxine has become less stalky nowadays too and Jamie takes a lot of her time – perhaps this would all work out and she would be happy just looking after him. Although I do sense he's more closely bonded to me than to her. It would be nice if she were more affectionate with him. It could all work out if Bella and I just come clean and tell everyone. We might all live happily ever after. It's a nice thought and I put ideas of killing people out of my mind, returning instead to thoughts of Bella waiting for me in a hotel room.

The Tale of Being Neighbourly

I'm fairly well conditioned to long-distance journeys, but twenty hours to Cairns is a very long drive. Thankfully the Jeep has a decent audio system and most of a tank of gas too. I did at least remember to draw plenty of cash so I should be fine to fuel up as needed along the way without the worry of having to use a bank card. The first thing to do is swap the number plates, so I pull over and unscrew some from a Hyundai. I will switch them back when I get back in forty-eight hours.

The first five hours of the journey go smoothly and I listen to some easy listening tunes, singing along whenever I recognise the song. I've a CD with me by The Wonder Stuff and I run through that too, particularly one track I have in mind for Jason. His own track, just for him – something to get me into the mood and I've been the mood for that bastard for years. I've also packed a few energy drinks in my rucksack so I still feel alert, but the fuel gauge is showing the tank's getting a bit low and you can quickly become stranded in Australia if you're not careful. The next town along the coastline I will come to is Rockhampton. I'll fuel up there and maybe even have a micro-nap.

It's practically midnight when I see the neon sign of a gas station on the approach to Rockhampton, so I pull over, fill up and buy a phone top-up card. The Jeep takes on plenty of fuel so it'll probably only need gassing up once more in Townsville, which is five hours south of Cairns.

As I drive out of the gas station, I look for a quiet place to try and call Maxine for a check-in and hopefully a short nap. Rockhampton is ever so slightly inland, but the Fitzroy River runs straight through the town centre and I spot a largely empty car park that looks dark on the edge of the river bank. This is crocodile country though, so I'll need to keep my distance. But it'll do nicely for a nap. Firstly though I top up the phone credit, change the settings to protect caller ID to hide my whereabouts and ring Maxine.

'I'm so pleased you called!' says Maxine. She sounds tense.

'Everything OK?' I ask.

'Yes, it is now – but I've been trying your hotel and getting no answer,' she says.

'Oh, that's weird. I'm calling from the hotel room now,' I say.

'Yes, weird – shall I call it again?'

'No, I'll report it tomorrow or just call you,' I say. It's difficult to shake off her stalker tendencies and her need to know where I am all the time.

'OK,' she says, unconvincingly. 'All going OK – Kamila and Lachlan looked after you?' she asks. It was interesting she never said she knew of my tryst with Kamila. It was as if nothing had ever happened. When I asked why they stopped visiting us she always brushed it off. It didn't sound too positive the way things had ended between her and Kamila. Kamila even sounded a bit scared. It made me think of Leighton and what he'd said about her, that she was crazy and sex was her idea to pay off her debt. Maxine never gave me that impression and I never pressed her on it.

We chat for a while, but I quickly get sleepy and she lets me go. In my experience, it's better to stay in contact with her as that avoids sudden appearances or more intrusive questions that I might not be able to reasonably answer. I tell her I'll call again tomorrow before I leave, then I set my alarm for 1.a.m. and recline the driver's seat. I fall asleep almost instantly and the next thing I know, my alarm is ringing. I yawn, stretch and get out of the car for a quick pee into the river. I guzzle down an energy drink and then get moving again, if a bit sluggishly.

By the time I make it to Townsville I've had another two energy drinks and a family pack of pick-n-mix. It's brighter now as morning is upon me and traffic starts to appear on the road. A quick check of the time on the dashboard and I see it's shortly after 7 a.m. It's such a boring journey from here, but it has at least afforded me some time to plan out how I will tackle Jason.

When eventually I make it to Cairns it's getting close to 1 p.m. I needed a few quick dashes to bushes on the roadside thanks to those damn energy drinks. They go straight through me, and the desire to urinate becomes overwhelming. It feels good to be in Cairns again, especially when I'm here for a good cause. It's interesting to feel the difference in air quality between here and Brisbane. The air is much thicker here, almost suffocating with humidity. When we lived in Cairns, I'd occasionally get a sense of panic at just how oppressive the air felt. I drive into the city centre district and park the SUV near the marina where there's a big open air car park. As I step from the car, my legs are all tingly from being in it so long. The area's already busy with tourists milling around the public lido and I feel like jumping in fully clothed to freshen up.

I grab an iced coffee from the lido shop, along with an 'I love Cairns' baseball cap that I pull down over my face in case anyone recognises me. I put on a vest and a pair of Rip Curl board shorts and then head to the pool. As I enter the water, my penis stings from friction burns after being with Kamila. God she was enthusiastic. But when the stinging subsides it's so refreshing to be in the pool after such a long and sweaty journey.

Having woken up after a swim, I sit on the grassy bank letting myself dry off and watching the tourists. They seem to be enjoying themselves and everything here is exactly as I remember it. It could have been just yesterday that we lived here and I close my eyes, remembering what it was like. I feel like driving back to our old house, expecting to see Jamie and Maxine there, but then images of Jason flood into my mind and reinvigorates me for my task ahead.

I turn my mind to looking at the map now, reminding myself where Jason's company head office is based. He's probably out somewhere installing equipment in the city – everywhere needs air conditioning here. After finishing another cool drink, I decide to drive to his office building and see if I can spot his car in the car park. I cruise past his building slowly but I'm disappointed that I can't see it anywhere. Perhaps he's bought a new one since we left? I decide to risk detection and take a drive out to Kewarra Beach, where we lived. It's the middle of the day so most people will be out at work. His wife was a hairdresser so I remember she had erratic work patterns. It's plausible she's at home, but I'm unlikely to be recognised in the borrowed Jeep and my bogan clothes.

Arriving on our old street, I see the same set of modern, one-storey sprawling family homes all with their lawns neatly presented on either side of the narrow cul-de-sac. It could be a set from the Australian soap, *Neighbours*. There was usually an asshole in that neighbourhood too. Well today, this one might just lose their asshole. The houses are so nicely spread out that you would think it would be impossible to be affected by something so mundane as noise from a neighbour. Suddenly it all seems such a lot of effort to go to just because someone played his music a bit too loud. But then I remember him flicking his middle finger at me and Jamie, his meanness towards Maxine when she was sick and I decide that I'll show him who can *really* be mean. I'm *meaner than mean*.

I drive up to his house slowly, but I'm troubled to see his boat isn't here and I start to feel a panic. Has he moved – I really did chance it by just coming here without a plan. I could have checked his whereabouts but decided against it as I had no room to make any alteration to these days on my work trip. It's possible that that he's out of town.

I turn the Jeep around at the foot of the cul-de-sac and again pass back slowly past the houses. I can't see anything distinctive at his house to indicate he still even lives there and I feel a bit stumped. Exiting the street disappointed, I curse that I haven't managed to locate him. It occurs to me he's probably taking a day off for a fishing trip. He always used to take his boat to the nearby Blue Water Marina to launch, rather than going all the way into the city. So I decide to take a drive over there to see if there is any sign of him.

Blue Water is a new housing estate built on an outshoot of the main estuary close to the northern beaches area of Cairns. People not wanting to permanently moor their boats tend to bring them here via trailers. They then reverse them into the water, leaving their vehicles in the car park until they're done.

Looking around the marina, I can see five trailers on a grass bank and a bunch of vehicles in the car park. Scanning along the cars I almost jump for joy when I see the familiar sight of his grey Toyota SUV. I feel instant relief and excitement. It's most likely he'll be gone for the rest of the day, returning around dusk along with the rest of the boating community. I look at my watch and see I have a couple of hours before he gets back. It would be too much good fortune to assume that he'll be alone, so I ought to prepare a plan to accommodate a few people being around. He usually goes with a mate or two, or sometimes with his family. So I park up nearby to watch the car park and consider my options.

Letting down Leighton's tyres worked well a few years ago and the same strategy could work here too if it slows down Jason's exit, isolating him from the pack. I get out of the Jeep and stroll over to his vehicle. No one's around and so I calmly release the air from all four of his tyres. With only an hour till dusk, I'm back in the Jeep, reclining in the driver's seat, waiting for his return.

The Present Tale

My phone rings and I can see it's Bella.

'Hi. Are you far away?' she asks.

'About an hour or so by the look of it,' I say. I have visions of her wearing a tight black PVC dress that we discussed her buying a while ago. I wonder if that is the surprise.

'I have a surprise for you,' she says, laughing.

'I know, I know, you said!' I say. She *must* have got the dress.

'I'll be ready and waiting for you then,' she says, sounding in a good mood. I think today I might suggest we get married, after we have sex of course. We'd obviously need to leave our partners, but love is love. It'll obviously come as a blow to her husband, but they haven't had sex in ages so he must know something like this is coming. Maxine's reaction could be problematic; I don't expect she would take it well. Trying to stay one step ahead of a stalker for all these years is frankly exhausting and I think it's time for a change. Time for something pure, innocent and loving in my life – time for Bella.

'Sounds great,' I say. I put my foot down on the accelerator to see if I can get there a bit quicker.

The next thirty minutes go smoothly enough until I hit roadworks. Curse my damn satnav – how did it not pick this up? It must have just happened as there's no sign of traffic lights and all I see is an emerging line of static cars. There are some workmen nearby in their high visibility jackets sitting down with mugs and a drinking flask in the layby. A couple of drivers ahead of me exit their cars to see what's happening. Perhaps they can speed things up – so I give a toot on my horn. One of them flashes a middle finger at me, which is not nice as I'd meant it supportively, but I'll let it slide on this occasion. I watch them walk over and berate the workmen, although the workmen seem unperturbed by this, pointing to their watches and continuing with their tea. It's probably their statutory tea-break. Bloody unions.

'Oh, come on, get on with it,' I hear one of the drivers shout. He looks pretty angry, but the workmen wave him away dismissively and carry on chatting. I'm in a hurry too, so I watch with interest and toot my horn again. I know a thing or two about violence and I would estimate one of the drivers is going to completely lose it soon. The workmen are much bigger men, but it's a hot day and the drivers are enraged. In my view, rage can win over size and this is one of the reasons I use music to find the balance of mood I want for a particular kill. It doesn't pay to be out of control; controlled rage is good though. One of the drivers looks like he's well beyond the state where music would be useful. It's a hot day so the heat will add to his agitation. I forget about Bella for a moment, sit back and watch it unfold.

I see the more annoyed driver return to his car. Some other drivers toot their horns now and so I join in again, content that I have some safety in numbers. Tooting horns are sure to add to the tension. Instead of climbing back into his driver's seat, he opens his trunk and pulls something out. I see him walk back towards the workmen with what looks very much like a golf club. I think it's a pitching wedge, either that or a nine iron.

He raises the club over his shoulder as he faces the workmen, shouting at them. The burlier of the two workers calmly passes his mug to the other. He doesn't seem flustered, so this probably happens to them quite a lot. He moves languidly towards the driver who makes a couple of false swings of the club. The chorus of horns from other drivers grows louder but I don't see anyone rushing in to break it up. The workmen look at each other and finally shrug, gesturing for the man to get back in his car. They throw the remains of their tea towards the grass verge and move back towards the road, removing the traffic cones that were blocking our lane. The driver is calming now and gets in his car. With a middle-fingered hand gesture to the workmen out of his window, he accelerates hard and the traffic moves off. That was fun, but it has just made me a further fifteen minutes late for Bella.

The rest of the journey is straightforward enough. Maxine calls me once to see when I will be home. I tell her it will be late this evening, so that saves me having to call her from the hotel with an update anyway. I multi-task and send Bella a text message to let her know I'll be there imminently. Now would be a good time for her to change into her new PVC outfit.

See you soon then. I will be ready – so excited! Hope you like the surprise!

She texts back instantly.

The Tale of Being Neighbourly

I jolt myself awake as I hear loud voices, and the sound of car engines in the car park. Have I overslept and missed Jason? It's dusk and I look around with bleary eyes – the long drive has really taken it out of me. People are now moving cars and trailers, making me panic for a moment as I scan the scene looking for him. Surely I can't have missed him. Looking at the grass verge there are no cars there at all now and some cars are leaving. I rub my sleepy eyes again, take another slug of an energy drink and look closely. Thankfully I see him. He's standing next to his SUV, scratching his head as his mate laughs. A couple of others are in conversation with them, but I don't recognise them, just him and his giggly mate. Jason's trailer is in the water with his boat on top of it. It looks like he is thinking how he can hook it up to his SUV which he's now noticed has four flat tyres. It won't get very far so he'll need to pump those up first. I watch him get a foot pump out of his trunk while one of the others kindly tows his boat from the water for him.

As Jason pumps the tyre with his foot, I see his mate bending down to check it's taking air and he gives a thumbs up, so Jason continues to pump. It'll be hard work to pump up all four of them but they spend the next ten minutes taking it in turns, which isn't handy – I was hoping he'd be alone doing this. Curse the neighbourly Aussies. I am not sure I could take on the both of them, but at least everyone else is leaving now. I'd fancy my chances with Jason and his puny biceps in any circumstances and especially aided by the element of surprise. He's younger than me and I expect he could put up a fight if I let him, but I'm fit. However, the baseball bat I bought for the occasion should sway the balance of any encounter. Nevertheless, if there are two of them, it could be tricky.

Just when I think it's going to be a frustrating evening, I get lucky as another SUV comes along. It's the wife of Jason's mate, coming to give him a lift home. They share a joke and wave goodbye to Jason. They'll come to remember that wave with some poignancy. Jason will be a while longer yet, and still has two and a half tyres to go. It's getting dark now too, so he must be becoming frustrated. I recline again and decide to wait a few minutes longer, so he can grow even more tired. I turn on the music system and listen to The Wonder Stuff. I've always meant to have a song of theirs on my list – my favourite band can now join the gang. But it's not one of their sunnier tracks today. It'll be no jolly song for Jason – there's no fun to be had, no frivolity, no playing around, not for Jason. Jason's going to suffer. I feel the need for a bit of menace today, something a bit 'Fee-fi-fo-fum, I smell the blood of an Australian'. I'm the giant in this story and I've found the perfect track for him. So I turn on the stereo, get myself in the mood for the kill and sing along to the first verse of 'Meaner Than Mean':

'Good grief said the thief when I cut off his hands
Oh the blood did run, oh the big blood did pour
Oh my, said the fly, when I pulled off his wings

Did you really have to do such a terrible thing.'

I feel myself start to transition into killing mood. Slow, methodical, ruthless and utterly unforgiving. I clench the bat tightly as I watch him trying to pump up his tyres. The chorus comes on and I mouth the words as my eyes stay transfixed on my prey.

'I'm mean, I'm mean, I'm meaner than mean

It takes all this hate to fuel my machine

I'm cruel, I'm cruel, I'm crueller than cruel

I'm meaner than mean and cooler than cool.'

Waiting until he starts the fourth tyre, I quietly slip out of the Jeep from my position across the road, singing the next verse to myself.

'No joke I took your hope, you'll hang from the rope

I'll kick over your chair and laugh when you choke

Oh dear came the cheer when I took away your life

One slip with my knife and out went your lights.'

I sing it under my breath, knowing every word as I twirl the baseball bat in my hand like a baton, taking a wide loop as I moonwalk up to Jason from behind. He's absorbed in what he's doing, although his foot pumping rate is now very slow. The surface of the car park is tarmacked and so he can't hear my light footsteps as I close in on him. 'I'm mean, I'm mean, I'm meaner than mean,' I sing out loud now and he momentarily looks at me as I swish the bat.

'I'm meaner than mean and cooler than cool,' I sing at full volume and swing the bat hard into the kneecap of his supporting leg. He cries out and I hear bone cracking, only slightly muffled by my singing, as he falls to the ground.

I swiftly raise the bat again and bring it down as he instinctively grabs his knee with both hands. I hear another crack of bone in his arm, attacking him now in a frenzy of excitement that's been building in me for so long. I don't stop until I'm sure I've disabled him, breaking or badly damaging both his arms and legs. When the mist clears from my mind and I look at him again I see him on the ground, crying in pain. His limbs look bloodied and awkwardly misaligned. I remember how this situation went with Leighton, so I stand watching him writhing on the floor, waiting for his pain levels to normalise.

'Hello Jason,' I say, calming myself and politely speaking to him when he stops screaming. 'It's been a while.'

In the dark he squints to look at me. Then I see a look of horror on his face as he realises who it is.

'You!' he cries.

'Yes,' I say, smiling.

'Please no,' he says.

I laugh, starting to feel the enjoyment rising in me again, the ecstasy of a kill – there's nothing that even gets close to matching this.

'Oh Jason, you've had this coming,' I say. As I raise the bat again, he tries to raise his broken arms up to protect his face, but they're both bent so awkwardly it makes me laugh and I put the bat down. But I didn't want this to be a fun encounter. This one is about making him suffer. I also can't hang around too long revelling in the moment, anyone could come by. I need to get back to my motel on the Sunshine Coast yet. I pause as my laughter has given him some encouragement that all might not be lost.

'That's better, let's talk about it, mate,' he says.

'Oh yes, what should we talk about?' I say, giving him a moment but noting time is tight.

'We can work something out. I mean I've always felt bad about things you know,' he says. I laugh again and shake my head.

'I just don't believe you,' I say.

'Please, please, I have a family,' he says and now I see real fear etched on his face.

'Not anymore,' I say, which makes me laugh again, despite myself. He doesn't seem to find the laughter so reassuring now.

This time instead of raising the bat, I bring out a transparent plastic freezer bag from my pocket and place it over his head. While he fumbles around with his flailing, bent and broken arms, I quickly seal it with parcel tape under his chin. He tries to grapple with it using his broken arms, which is just hilarious. Does he not realise I'm trying to take this kill seriously.

I lean in towards him, watching his face through the bag and I can see him grimace, unable to find the strength or control of his limbs to remove it. After thirty seconds, the front of the bag become suctioned to his face as he devours the last remnants of air. I gaze at him as he reaches for his final gasps, staring at me, panicked and flailing his arms, trying to rip at the bag. But then he stops moving and is still. He falls flat to the tarmac and I leave him for a couple of minutes next to his Toyota, watching him before I carefully cut the tape and remove the bag from his head.

Once I'm finished, I drag him by his feet to the water's edge and then roll him in to the estuary. I watch him semi submerge face down in the water and I stay there until I see him float out from the edge. The saltwater crocodiles and tiger sharks in the area will find him soon enough and should enjoy a tasty evening feed.

Getting back into the Jeep I check myself over. I look clean enough and the use of the bag was a good idea to finish him off – Leighton had been messy and that was a lesson learned. This was much cleaner; a bit of local tissue trauma on Jason's arms and legs when I incapacitated him, but no blood spurting everywhere, more about blunt trauma and internal wounds. It was just so much better executed than Leighton and I feel happy about this as a new protocol moving forward – good job. Well done, me.

★★★

The drive back to the Sunshine Coast is uneventful but I'm happy now a weight has been lifted, so time goes much more quickly than on the way to Cairns. I visualise the moments where Jason had annoyed both Maxine and I, then fast forward to the images of him drawing his last breaths, frantically trying to rip the bag from his head with his smashed arms. It brings a pleasant tingle of excitement down my spine.

I'm so absorbed in the events that I manage the trip with only two stops to grab a sandwich, a couple more energy drinks and to take on some fuel. At 1 a.m. I unscrew some new plates from a Toyota I find parked on a quiet section of road near Townsville and put them on the Jeep for the remainder of the journey.

I push on to Rockhampton and get there just after 6 a.m. Then finally I arrive on the Sunshine Coast at 2 p.m., exhausted but glad I've made it. I pull off the road on the outskirts of town, change the plates back to the originals, throw the Toyota plates in the bush and head into town, looking for a convenient place to abandon the Jeep. My flight back to Heathrow leaves later this evening and so I have time to relax for a while at the motel – maybe get some sleep too.

There's a service station near the beach and I think about being a good citizen and filling the tank of the Jeep, but I'm not sure if they have CCTV and it's a risk too far so I decide against it. It's been a good vehicle for sure and I will remember that the next time I'm in the market for a new car. Would it be too cute to return the Jeep to where I found it? That's perhaps too risky – but I see a parking spot on the main street and my motel is only a twenty-minute walk from here. So I take a calculated risk, quickly rub down the steering wheel with some alcohol wipes, collect my debris together into the kill bag and dispose of my rubbish in a roadside skip. Hopefully the police will return the Jeep to the owners and there will be no need for too close an inspection. There's no damage, just a lot of extra kilometres – no reason to delay returning it to them. So I pull down my baseball cap, grab my bag and close the car door behind me, leaving the keys in the ignition as I found them.

When I arrive back at my motel room, I'm relieved to be here in one piece. I close the door behind me, throw my bag on the bed and sigh. I may just have gotten away with this and that gives me an immense sense of satisfaction. I run a hot shower and then, after towelling myself dry, lie on the bed, curling up in a comfy foetal position to get some well-earned sleep. I need to be at Brisbane airport in five hours, so I have time for a good nap. My alarm is set for 5.30 p.m. and I go straight to sleep. But at 5 p.m. I wake suddenly, being violently shaken.

'Where the hell have you been?' says Kamila.

The Tale of Being Neighbourly

By the time I board my plane, I am unbelievably sore from having to penetrate Kamila again. I was barely recovered from our first bout and so tired, but I needed to placate her somehow and that seemed the best way. I had to push through the pain barrier, but now on the plane I discreetly make my way to the on-board loo to apply a soothing, topical cream which thankfully helps a bit. The pharmacist sounded more amused than concerned when I explained the problem at the airport. What an asshole.

I had to promise to give Kamila a full explanation of where I'd been, although I don't yet have any idea what that explanation will be. As I thrust myself into her, I'd been wracking my brain to find some explanation.

'But darling, where on earth were you?' she said when we finished.

'Just walking – trying to clear my head, Kamila. I couldn't stop thinking about you,' I said. It was the best I could do at the time – make it about her.

'Oh darling, I feel the same,' she said, hugging me like a bear cub, causing me a great deal of discomfort, particularly my poor penis. It was a miracle I managed to climax while I was in such pain. I just closed my eyes and thought of Bella.

'Yes, but you have Lachlan and I have Maxine,' I said to Kamila, acknowledging the impossibility of our unrequited love. She hugged me even tighter.

'Oh sweetie, it will be OK,' she said, still clinging to me.

'We will have to be star-crossed lovers, never destined to be fully together.' I heard someone say something that in a movie once and I almost vomited. Clearly Kamila likes that sort of thing as she still clinged to me.

'I came here yesterday in the middle of the night, Jez dear and you weren't here. I was so worried,' she says.

'Yes, I was walking on the beach contemplating things.'

'Oh, to think, you were out there pining for me.'

'Yeah, that's what I was doing.'

'Oh, you poor dear.'

She carries on hugging and talking to me about the meaning of true love. I considered whether I should kill her. No one would know she was visiting me, certainly she wouldn't have told Lachlan – it could be cleaner if I just killed her. It would stop her talking at least. But someone on the motel staff had obviously let her into my room, so I ruled this out as a serious option and she carried on chattering.

'Oh, Jez darling, I have dreamed of this,' she says, squeezing me again and this time stroking my crotch with her hand.

'This needs to remain our secret until we are ready to tell people, my dear Kamila,' I say, moving her hand.

I dozed for a moment and when I wake she's still talking, planning out our future together. It seemed to go on for eternity until I could make the excuse that I needed to get to the airport.

When we get to the terminal, she hugs me again. 'Jez, I love you and think I always have,' she says. I give her a kiss on the cheek and feel like patting her on the head much as one might with a puppy. It was nice she drove me to the terminal, but I also still need to clear security, pick up a present for Jamie and walk to the executive lounge to get properly loaded on the complimentary champagne.

'Yes, me too. It's only ever been about you Kamila,' I say, walking through security to a souvenir shop I spotted.

'I'll find a way to come to you. I will make it right with Maxine!' she shouts after me. I see some people around me smile; they must think she's a nutter and they're not wrong. I nod back, give her a little wave and speed up.

The complimentary champagne is a bit flat in the Executive Lounge, which is disappointing and, worse still, access to it is limited, which always strikes me as a bit cheap. But after four glasses I'm beginning to feel pleasantly mellow and ready to undertake the twenty-four-hour flight back to the UK.

When I arrive at Heathrow, I can see Maxine waiting for me at the arrivals gate. She doesn't look completely happy and there's no sign of Jamie.

'Missed you,' she says, giving me a hug, but still frowning at me.

'Everything alright?' I ask.

'I'm not sure – is it?' she says. It makes me wary when she's like this. Suspicion leads to me being followed and more intrusion. That means a pause in my hobbies and so it's best to keep Maxine happy and unsuspecting.

'Yes, everything's fine – just so tired. I barely slept,' I say.

'It's just you didn't call me again,' she says. I realise I got so busy with Jason and with Kamila so I didn't manage to call her back.

'Ah sorry. Yes, I slept a lot,' I say.

'I thought you said you didn't get any sleep?' she says.

'On the plane I mean. I didn't sleep on the plane,' I say. I see Jamie in the distance, coming out of the loo and I break clear of Maxine to walk towards him.

I watch him for a moment before he notices I'm there. He smiles when he picks me out in the crowd and runs towards me. It's a cross between a walk and run as he tries not to look too uncool – I hold out my arms as he does a last little dash towards me and I give him a hug. I smell his baby scent as I swing him in the air.

'My boy,' I say, giving him a kiss on the head. As I put him down, I ruffle his hair.

'Daaad,' he says, protesting. I hand him his present in a little bag and he jumps up and down excitedly. 'Can I open it now?!'

'Go on then,' I say and Maxine tuts at me disapprovingly. She has never really understood the bond between father and son. He opens the bag and looks perplexed for a moment.

'What is it?' he asks.

'It's a shark tooth necklace. It's a sign of great strength to wear it. It's very manly and yet it's good luck too,' I say. Maxine shakes her head; I imagine she can guess it was a last-minute present from the airport gift shop.

'I'm never taking it off,' says Jamie. He is such a sweet boy.

Maxine drives us home while Jamie chatters away in the back of the car, playing with his new necklace before becoming engrossed in a game on his phone.

'Did much happen while I was away?' I ask Maxine when he settles down.

'Not too much. You've done everything you needed?' she asks. If only she knew what I had done, and I half wish I could tell her about my adventure with Jason. Telling her about it would bring her into my private business and mean I could never really leave her. All she knows about is Tommy and that was such a long time ago it barely counts. That was a one-off in her mind.

'Yes, it was very successful,' I say, remembering Jason's lifeless body floating face down in the marina.

'Good. Was Kamila OK?' she asks.

'Yes, she and Lachlan were on good form,' I say. But Maxine remains silent for a moment.

'I ask because she just called me to say she's planning to come for a visit,' says Maxine.

'Oh yes?'

'Yes.' She sounds suspicious. I try not to look concerned, but this could be inconvenient.

'That'll be nice,' I say.

'Did they say anything about it while you were there?'

'Not really.'

'She sounded a bit weird,' says Maxine. I start to regret my strategy of playing along with Kamila's romantic vision for us. I thought she was just fantasising.

'Weird?'

'Nothing odd happened when you were there?' I'm sure Maxine shoots me a look, but I could be mistaken.

'Not that I can think of,' I say.

'She really didn't say she was coming?' she asks. I shake my head, but it feels like I've chosen the wrong option of how to answer this question.

'Well, she says she has something important to discuss

with me,' says Maxine. My heart sinks as she says this. I'm getting on so well with Bella that I could really do without this complication.

'Did she say what it was?' I ask.

'No, she wouldn't expand on it,' says Maxine as she takes a roundabout too fast.

The Present Tale

I arrive at the hotel Bella has booked for us. It's discreetly placed on the edge of town, with good parking, and so neither of us are likely to be recognised. I pull into the car park and see her Ford Focus is already there.

I park a safe distance from her car, grab my jacket from the backseat, put it on and head to the reception to collect a pass key for the room. With the key card in hand, I make my way to the lift and head up to the room.

I swipe the pass key down the chip reader on the door and the door clicks as it unlatches. I push it gently open and let myself in.

The room is dark – she's thoughtfully closed the drapes and there is only a single lamp for light in corner, by the double bed. I can make out the bed in the dim light and see it's untouched, with two sets of towels still in place upon it, each with a wrapped chocolate on top. I take one, unwrap it and pop it in my mouth. But the light to the far side of the room is very low and I can't see Bella.

'Bella?' I call out, squinting to adjust my eyes to the dim lighting. She doesn't answer but as they become accustomed to the dark, I can now make out her shape on the far side of the room – what *is* she doing? As my eyes acclimatise, I see her kneeling in front of an armchair. I can't make out why, or what it is she's doing, but disappointingly whatever she's doing, she's not doing it in a PVC dress. It looks like she is in her lacy black slip – that's a good look anyway. I can now make out the peachy shape of her bottom, but her head is nestled in the chair. As my eyes normalise, I see her head properly now and it's moving slowly up and down.

'Bella?' I whisper, feeling suddenly panicked. But she ignores me and I see her head continue to move, accompanied now by familiar groaning noises of pleasure. As I stand frozen to the spot, I hear a deeper groan from another voice – a man. I'm unable to move and now chewing my complimentary chocolate feels impossible as my mouth becomes dry. She raises her head, smiling at me, but the man places his hands on either side of her head to push her back down and she submits. I see his hands relax as he reclines in the chair. I stand staring at them, my vision better, now seeing the scene but not knowing what to do, so I just stay where I am. Then I see her withdraw from him once again, getting to her feet now despite his protests. She walks over to me slowly.

'Bella?' I say.

'Shhhh' she says putting a finger to my lips as she approaches me. Her breasts are tumbling from the front of her slip. My stomach is churning and I suppress vomit. I start to protest but she drops to her knees whispering, 'Just relax,' as she unbuckles my belt. I look over to the armchair and can see the man looking at us and stroking himself. As I fully see his face, I recognise it's her husband.

She tenderly kisses my groin and like a reflex action I can feel myself quickly getting hard. 'I am not sure about this,' I say as she takes me in her mouth and I lose myself for a moment. She looks up at me, seeing I am looking over at her husband.

'He wanted to join us today,' she says smiling.

'I didn't think he knew?' I whisper.

'He's always known,' she says and shrugs. They share a smile before she lowers her head again. I feel a wave of pleasure build up inside that revolts me. He's stroking himself vigorously now as she also works up a faster rhythm. I grab her head forcefully with my hands to take control. She groans as she had earlier and I try to close my mind to it, but then I hear him too. I slow down for a moment and she briefly gasps for air.

'Come for me, Jez,' she says and then puts me back in her mouth groaning even louder. I feel myself approach climax but then something tells me to stop and I pull away. I look down at her, across to her husband, then over to the corkscrew by the kettle. I could skewer both of them with it – it would be so easy, they wouldn't have a chance. But for some reason I can't do it.

'No,' I say. I rebuckle my trousers and rearrange myself.

'Jez, this can be fun – a new way of life for the three of us,' she says. Her husband is standing now, facing us both with his erect penis. I can't help but look for a moment. Thankfully I notice that I'm definitely bigger.

'Go to hell,' I say and leave the room.

The Present Tale

It's morning and I wake, stretch but then I remember the previous evening in the hotel with Bella and her husband. I feel like never getting up again and dive back under the duvet. Maxine brings me a cup of coffee when I show no sign of stirring and settles herself in bed with me, telling me her plans for the weekend. I nod distractedly in agreement, sip the coffee and stare at my phone on the side table wondering if I should look to see if I have any messages from Bella.

'Are you OK?' asks Maxine when she stops speaking. I see I've spilt some coffee on my T-shirt.

'Yes, alright. Just slipped,' I say as I put the mug down.

'It's just your hand is shaking,' she says.

'No it isn't,' I snap back.

'OK,' she says, quietly taking a sip of her tea. When she's not looking, I take a look at my hand and see it's trembling hard. I feel cold, shiver, and climb deeper under the bed covers. 'You're not well,' she says, feeling my brow. I grunt in agreement with her.

'I might stay in bed,' I say. I'm feeling nauseous. 'Do we have any paracetamol?'

'I'll get some,' she says, jumping up from the bed before coming back with a fresh packet from the bathroom. Maxine would never betray me like that, that's one thing about marrying your stalker. I take two pills and she leaves me to sleep but I can't. I can't get Bella out of my mind and I check my phone when Maxine leaves the room. I see there are twenty messages. I notice she didn't send the first message until an hour or so after I left the hotel. I imagine she finished him off first and I feel sick. I thought she was mine. You can't expect a serial killer to be a sharer. I delete all the messages without reading them and put the phone down so I can try to sleep.

When I wake again it's almost midday. I sit up in bed and Don is on my mind now. Would I have killed him if it hadn't been for Bella? I think not; I wouldn't have risked the prospect of jail but for her.

★★★

I decide to try and enjoy the rest of the weekend by spending time with Jamie. I should divert some of the time I usually spend obsessing over Bella on being a better father. Maybe he can be my focus now. I know he has a football match this afternoon, so I tell him he need not do a car share with his teammate today and I'll take him. He seems pleased by this and chatters away happily all the way there, which proves a good distraction.

I get into the spirit of the game quickly. 'That was offside!' I shout at the referee as the game barely gets underway. Several parents nod at me in agreement, although I'm clearly being biased – there is no way it was offside. The opposition look very good today and it appears Jamie could be in for a heavy beating. I really wish he wasn't so awful. It's quickly three-nil to the other team inside the first fifteen minutes and is still at that score when the referee blows the whistle for half-time.

Jamie and his teammates all run over to the coach for some words of wisdom. I wonder if they realise they're hopeless? It's sweet really I guess – they seem happy enough and that's the main thing. Some of the parents are chatting, but I'm not feeling very sociable on the side of the pitch today. I normally fit in quite well and I do enjoy football; it's one of those male bonding sports that mean you can quickly establish social groups and easy conversation either as a player or as a parent. Some mums get involved but not too many. Mostly it's still a male environment although it's always nice when there's female company here.

I barely think about Bella during the game, although I realise I need to figure out how to properly get her off my mind for good. Should I kill her and her husband? I've done worse in the past and I could do that – it might help, but I feel too sad to properly think it through at the moment. I doubt I'd even enjoy it. It'd be like eating a favourite meal when you've lost your sense of taste. I need to get my taste back before I do anything.

I consider my other immediate options and the first one that comes to mind is to simply go out and find another woman to take her place. Thinking about it, I get stomach cramps and have to crouch down – what's wrong with me? Is it possible that I could I simply share Bella with her husband. Would that work? I doubt it – I thought she and I were the team but she obviously thought differently. At the very least she's deceived me and was still sexually active with him – was she with Don I wonder? Maybe she used me, but I doubt she knows what I am. If she knew my true nature, she would not have been so stupid as to bring her husband to the hotel.

'Good game,' I shout, clapping as the final whistle goes and the boys run off the pitch. It's full-time already and I barely registered the second half of the game at all.

'What was the final score?' I ask our centre forward's dad, Jimmy. He's normally a talkative fella but looks a bit sullen. I'm not sure whether it's the score or the absence of his wife from the sideline today that's upsetting him.

'Five-nil. A thrashing,' he says, shaking his head. 'Bloody useless.'

Five-nil is quite a loss – although in reality that's not too bad. It looked like it could have been a real hiding when I was paying attention in the first half. The coach looks pleased – an exercise in damage control keeping it down to five. I see Jamie is still puffing; he has rosy cheeks as he stands in a circle around the coach getting their debrief. He could lose a few pounds – maybe I should take him for a run now and again. I give him a wave but he looks away – I must be an embarrassing parent.

'Your boy did OK,' says Jimmy. I can tell he's lying as Jamie is rubbish, as any casual observer could tell. However, this is a well-tried social strategy to initiate a process of reciprocal praise for your own child.

'Oh, he did OK, but your boy Connor held the team together in the second half,' I say, although this is simply an educated guess as I've barely watched the game at all. Jimmy's face lights up.

'Do you think so?' he says. If any of our team were actually any good then it would be Connor. If it gives his dad a nice compliment to share with his kid on their way home then why not. I do owe him one anyway.

'Yes, I think he has real potential,' I say, walking with

Jimmy towards the car park. His demeanour has perked up no end with that compliment as his wife arrives in their car. She waves when she spots us and I notice she flicks her hair. We had sex a while ago at one of those fundraising events for the boys' team. It was a slow night; we were there without our partners and we decided to escape the crowd for a bit, going for a late-night walk. So we had some fun on the seventh green of the local golf course which was pleasantly diverting. I look at her and she smiles back. I must say, she looks pretty hot today – maybe she could be a new project? If life were only that simple it would be nice. One out, one in – but Bella was a bit special. I stroll towards the car to wait until Jamie has showered and changed clothes.

Sitting in the driver's seat waiting, I turn on the radio. I haven't even thought too much about Don today, but I tune in to hear if there's any more coverage about him on local radio. I think again about my lost watch and it's starting to panic me. If it were found near the scene, enough people know I wear an Omega Moonwatch and my prints would be all over it. It could all unravel from there – it would be such a stupid way to be caught out. That's the thing about crime, none are perfect. If you've committed any kind of a crime then anything other than the absolute truth is an imperfection waiting to be found, somehow or other.

No one would ever start out expecting a middle-aged university professor to be a psychopathic serial killer, but once they did, all the pieces would fall into place and patterns would emerge that could trap me.

I see Jamie now as he walks towards me, chattering excitedly with his teammates. Can I be a true psychopath if I care so much about him? I think perhaps I might die for him, so am I really that bad? Perhaps I simply enjoy killing – is that so wrong or abnormal – I should not have to shoehorn myself into a dictionary definition. I'm more complex than some generic definition dreamed up by an academic.

Nothing about Don comes on the radio and I turn it off. Jamie's still saying goodbye to a couple of his teammates but soon comes to the car.

'Well played sunshine,' I say as he lets himself into the passenger seat next to me.

'Think so?' he asks, clipping his seat belt in place.

'Oh yes,' I say, starting the engine.

Maxine is cooking a stew when we get back. 'Did you win?' she asks. Jamie grunts. I nudge him and he rolls his eyes at me. We've spoken about this before and he needs to make more effort to engage with his mum.

'OK!' he whispers to me, slouching his shoulders and unnecessarily dragging his feet as he walks towards her. I leave them to chat.

I settle on to the sofa and flick on the TV. Another option for my future comes to mind: that I could just try to be a better husband and father. Would that be so bad? But then why do I still feel I need more than this? My stomach starts cramping again as I think of Bella.

The Present Tale

After another fruitless search of the house for my watch I'm feeling totally stressed out. It could be anywhere from Don's office on Drake's campus, in his car, the woods, somewhere in the house or at my flat near work in Ormskirk. It was so careless of me at a critical time but my mind had been racing trying to arrange the kill in a much shorter timeframe than usual. It was a panicked kill in response to his harassment of Bella and I could be about to pay the price for that.

Did I take it off as I buried him? Sometimes I do that when my wrists ache when using a shovel, but I just can't remember. That would be the worst-case scenario. I'm trying to remember when I last wore it, but I do tend to rely more on my phone for timekeeping these days, so there are big gaps in between where I might notice it's missing. Nevertheless, looking for it is at least diverting my attention away from thoughts of Bella. I'm only checking my phone for her messages every thirty minutes or so now, trying to reduce the frequency at which I look for them. I'm currently deleting them all instantly as they arrive so I imagine she will give up before long.

Aside from what to do about Bella and that husband of hers, I have two pressing issues. Whether or not to retrace my steps to find the missing watch, and also how to handle Terry Peak. Both are urgent for different reasons. Regarding the watch, I'm loathe to be seen in the vicinity of where I buried Don. That would be such a rookie-killer error. So I think I might leave that for another week and see if the watch turns up naturally without incriminating myself in a panic – it's probably somewhere around the house. My priority should be to develop a plan for Peak if I want to ensure I get the DVC post. I could just kill him once he's in post anyway, but then everyone would know he was picked for the job over me. That would do my ego no good whatsoever and I couldn't stand that. It would be better to either kill him pre-emptively before he's confirmed in the role, just as I had done with Tommy, or else somehow trip up his possible anointment to the role. I return to the kitchen to make myself a highball and consider the matter more closely. Jamie has now finished debriefing Maxine on his football exploits and is eating a Kit Kat. Chocolate won't help him run any faster around the pitch.

'You want one?' I ask Maxine as I pour the bourbon into my glass.

'Yes please!' she says. She starts retelling me about the match and how well Jamie played.

'Yes, I know. I was there,' I say.

'Oh yes of course!' she says. He's told her quite a tale about his exploits and not entirely factually it seems.

I spend the rest of the evening occupied with thoughts of what I should do about Terry Peak but not getting very far after two more highballs and then a couple of glasses of a rather decent single malt whisky. I'm completely relaxed and while not able to concentrate on the micro details I instead contemplate the bigger picture. If getting over Bella means throwing myself more into my career, then

I'd better make a success of it, and getting rid of Peak is therefore essential. I'll then be one step closer to being a VC, too.

'How's work these days?' asks Maxine as she settles into her favourite old armchair now that Jamie has headed to bed. I wish she would throw that chair out, it smells. Her waters broke in it and I'm not sure we've ever had it properly cleaned. It really irritates me and I never sit there.

'It's OK,' I say. I would normally limit my conversation with her, but I don't have Bella to chat with anymore, which feels weird so I decide to talk with Maxine. 'There might be an opportunity for a promotion.'

'Really? That's wonderful, Jez,' she says.

'It's not certain – it's between two of us and they'll make a decision next week,' I say.

'That's exciting. I know they will pick you!' she says. One thing about Maxine is her loyalty. She would never do what Bella did.

'I hope so,' I say.

'Is everything alright?' she asks. Her uncanny stalking senses must be tingling – she knows me too well. Actually, everything is not alright; I'm mourning that I will never see Bella's perky breasts ever again. I feel cramping pains return to my stomach.

'I'm alright, just a bit under the weather,' I say. This much is true; I notice I'm shivering again. 'I think I might go to bed.'

'That sounds sensible. You look terrible, poor dear. I'll bring you some honey and lemon,' she says. As she gets up, she crosses the room to kiss me on my forehead. I can smell the stench of the chair on her as she approaches me.

I undress and get into bed, forcing my mind to focus on Peak and make increased efforts to forget Bella. I imagine what I would like to do to Peak and this perks me up – but I'll need to think with greater clarity on this tomorrow, not now.

'Want a cuppa, Dad?' asks Jamie, popping his head around the door.

'I thought you were in bed?' I say.

'I can't sleep – been thinking about whether I should turn professional.'

'Professional?' I ask.

'At football,' he says.

'Ah yes, maybe,' I say. It's good to have dreams however unlikely they may be.

'Yes, we were talking about it today and… ' he starts to get very excitable.

'Go to bed!' I say. His shoulders slump and he heads off. I curl into a foetal position under the covers and try to keep my mind on Peak, not Bella. But I'm drawn magnetically to my phone and I reach out from under the covers to the side table where it's sitting.

'Can't you leave that bloody phone alone!' says Maxine, as I hear her come in and place a mug down on the table. I can smell the honey and lemon and it makes me feel pleasantly sleepy.

'I will,' I say.

'Hmmm. Get some sleep,' she says and leaves. For such an effective stalker it's a wonder she's never suspected Bella. But then Bella was always super careful, bordering on pathologically neurotic, in case we were caught.

I check for messages under the bed covers and I can see

another tranche of them from Bella. I want to hit delete again, but I feel too weak and drunk on whisky this evening so I decide to read them instead.

So sorry, Jez. We hoped you would be into it – I love you both and I want us all to be happy!

How can I make it up to you?

I didn't know how to tell you Mike and I still have sex – I'm so sorry it went wrong!

Please answer – he is completely cool about having an open relationship if it makes me happy. I can't leave him while he is so ill and I just want us all to be happy.

We could all be so happy together.

Why don't we try it again?

Or just you and me for a while until you are ready, whatever you prefer.

Please call me!!!!

I get this far and decide to delete the rest. Does she not realise that the thought of sharing is not in the psyche of a serial killer. The thought of her with him makes me feel sick. I travelled to Australia and drove twenty hours back and forth to Cairns just because Jason waved a middle finger at me. Imagine what I want to do to Mike after he waved his penis at me. So it's definitely in the interests of her and her husband to leave me alone. I try to remain calm, so I don't overreact, but thoughts of killing Mike are becoming difficult to control. So it's better I focus on my career, although admittedly even that choice likely involves killing someone.

The Present Tale

I wake at 3 a.m. and see my untouched honey and lemon drink on the bedside table. I reach over to it and take a sip. It's cold but alright. My mind's clearing from the effects of highballs and single malt whisky, so I turn again to Peak and what to do to him before David makes his recommendation on Thursday.

I still have the Taser hidden away that I used on Don. That was a useful acquisition and as a disabling strategy it was terrific, meaning I didn't have to get too close to him. The problem with the Taser of course is that it leaves visible puncture marks when the electrodes hit the body, breaking the skin. So that's a detectable method that could be seen as idiosyncratic and so I ought to use it sparingly. I could perhaps use it again in the right circumstances but only as a back-up. I don't want to end up with some ridiculous title like the Taser Killer or the Taser Torturer. How belittling it would be to have a nickname. For now, I should come up with a definite plan about what to do with Peak by Tuesday at the latest. Nothing is coming to me yet, but I'll travel to USL tomorrow and make some plans for him when I'm there, quietly on my own.

★★★

On Monday morning I head into the USL campus still with no firm plan for Peak formed in my mind. I've brought the

Taser and a big kitchen knife in my gym bag although I have no idea how I might use them. It just seemed a good idea to at least have some preparation. I'm running out of time and David will be in the process of making up his mind if he hasn't already. I hang my jacket on the peg of my office door and start up my computer.

'Morning Jez,' says Faye, breezing into my office without knocking. If she wasn't so attractive, I think I would kick her ass right out. It annoys me when people don't knock, even if they are hot as hell.

'Morning,' I say, abruptly and logging in to my email account without looking at her.

'Fancy a coffee?' she says. She obviously wants something. I look at my wrist to tell the time and remember I have a missing Omega issue, which doesn't help my mood. Maybe a coffee would be good – I glance quickly in her direction now and see she's undoing a button and pushing up her cleavage as she stands over my shoulder. She has some nerve, I'll give her that. She's obviously using her sexuality to get what she wants. If I engage with her does that make me the predator? I'm sure it'd cheer me up, but I'm not much in the mood.

I take another glance at Faye now that she's caught my attention and I notice her skirt is surely far too tight to be comfortable. I imagine her pert bottom bent over my desk and think perhaps that would drag me out of this depressive state. Justine told me she'd done things before to get her way. It would be a wriggle to lift her skirt though.

'Sure, yes, a coffee would be nice,' I say, giving up on my Jedi mind control skills as I try to use the force to make her to bend over the desk. Some things are best left in movies. We wander down to the senior common room together while she talks to me about something she did at the weekend. She's about as dull as Kamila.

The usual bunch of academics are in the common room. Mostly the ones who complain about being the busiest, yet they're still the ones with the most time available for coffee breaks. I let Faye queue up to get the drinks and I take up ownership of a small cluster of chairs near to where the politics staff team is seated. They always have time for coffee but are apparently ever so busy even though they have almost no students. What they are busy on remains a mystery.

As ever they are talking to each other on issues of international importance. They talk at the perfect volume for others in the surrounding area to hear and to be impressed. It's only when they have something of real interest to discuss that they whisper.

'Can I join you, Jez?' I look over and see the purple nose and rotund belly of Paul, the historian. I groan internally and see he's holding a mug in his clammy fist and smiling at me. It looks such an unnatural expression it starts to make me shiver. What the hell does he want?

'Yes, sure Paul. That would be nice,' I lie.

I think back to him and his colleagues visiting me in my office to complain about their lack of research excellence and I feel like taking his mug, swinging it into the back of his head, watching it shatter on impact and leaving fragments of his brain over the furniture.

'Had a good weekend, Paul?' I ask cheerily as he squeezes his fat backside into one of the armchairs. He doesn't hear me amid the effort of wiggling himself into the chair with a deep exhalation of breath. He's still smiling at me as if someone has given him a lobotomy. I do wonder how people like him ever survive in the world outside of academia. I only see people like Paul in the microcosm of university life and it's strange to think they do other things too. Perhaps they don't, they simply don't exist anywhere else, just here in an academic Brigadoon. Thankfully Faye arrives with the coffee and I quickly begin talking with her so Paul won't dominate the conversation with whatever it is he's smiling about. This is why I don't like coming for coffee – everyone wants something.

'So how are things, Jez?' says Paul ignoring my conversation with Faye. You have to love academics – no manners whatsoever. I turn and smile.

'Oh, not too bad Paul, thanks for asking,' I say and to his obvious irritation I start rattling off a long list of my weekly activities before he can do the same.

After ten minutes of tedious chit-chat, Paul tells me he has won a small research grant. I am both surprised and ever so slightly impressed by the old windbag. No wonder he was smiling – I bet he couldn't believe his luck. Faye looks bored as she hasn't yet had the chance to impress me, which I think is the purpose of our coffee. Before she gets the opportunity, Terry Peak appears with a couple of colleagues and I swear the ceiling lights flicker for a moment as he enters the room. It adds to the eerie menace of the situation or it is indicating a change in the force. Perhaps the dark side has entered the room. He can't know how close to death he is, or he wouldn't look so pleased with himself. I see him greet someone from the law school with a hearty pat on the shoulder. His familiar, fake belly laugh echoes from the other side of the room and my skin crawls once again. There's a spare fork lying on a plate in the returned cutlery bay and I contemplate walking up to him and poking it into his eye. Just as I am fantasising about this, we catch sight of each other before both quickly glancing away.

'You alright, Jez?' says Faye, interrupting my train of thought.

'Hmm?' I say, turning towards her. She's looking at me oddly. 'You look lost in thought – busy day ahead or is something wrong?'

'Oh sorry, all good – I was thinking about my next meeting,' I say, trying to carry off a casual smile, before taking a sip of my coffee.

I listen as Paul directs a new conversation about his interest in the battle of Agincourt to Faye and she nods agreeably to him. I recline in my armchair to finish my coffee, peacefully ignoring them both, but I'm interrupted by a sweaty hand patting the shoulder of my Hugo Boss suit jacket.

'Hi, Jez, great to see you,' says a familiar voice. I look up and see Peak grinning. I could twist his wrist from my shoulder and break his arm. I smile at him.

'You too, Terry, good to see you,' I say.

'Hey, Faye, how you doing?' says Peak, licking his toad-like lips.

'Hi, Terry, great thank you,' says Faye, fastening up the buttons of her blouse.

'You know the annual call for promotions came out this morning?' he says in her direction.

'Yes, I'd heard that,' she says, reddening.

'Got your application in yet? Or is that what you are tapping up Jez about this morning?' He bellows out another laugh and looks around the room for an audience.

'No, of course not,' she says, blushing further. I would have thought she was too brazen to blush – she's an interesting character after all. So now I understand the purpose of our coffee today.

'Just kidding. You totally deserve it,' he says. I'm not sure how he would know about her academic performance – he's in a different faculty.

'I do deserve it,' says Faye, as she gains composure. I see Peak licking his lips again and I realise he is busy trying to stare between the buttons of her blouse. He sees me noticing this and laughs again.

'She totally deserves it, if you know what I mean, Jez,' he says quietly, leaning in towards my ear. As he straightens back up, he lets out another of his belly laughs. Faye looks away from him and tuts, then starts a conversation with Paul.

'Big announcement due later this week then?' I say to Peak. He fixes me with his broad smile, and blinks at me in the way I imagine a toad might.

'Ah you've had the conversation with David, too?' he asks.

'Yes, last week,' I say. His fixed smile doesn't waver, and he blinks once more.

'Oh, I had my chat with him last month, but at least you're better late than never,' he says, patting my shoulder again, laughing. I look to see if the fork in the returned cutlery bay is within easy reaching distance. 'But seriously,

Jez, if they choose you, I will have no problem working for you,' he says. He blinks, toad-like, again.

'You too Terry,' I say. If I can't kill him, the first thing I will do is sack him, but for now I just smile instead. He pats my shoulder again as he moves off to join the rest of his group. I bet his sweaty hand has left a greasy mark.

Faye leans in towards me when he's gone and Paul is now engrossed in conversation with the politics team. 'Terry's such a creep,' she says.

I can't resist a smile and she instantly goes up in my estimation. Maybe she could get that promotion after all. I'd forgotten it was due to be advertised today and it makes sense that this is the sudden reason for her taking me for a coffee. We finish our drinks and she doesn't raise the topic again. She's looking very hot today though; I can see her nipples protruding slightly from her lace bra underneath her white blouse. The bright florescent lighting of the room is making it pleasantly transparent.

With Peak and now Faye to occupy my attention I've barely thought about Bella this morning. Maybe Faye could be a useful distraction for me. As I ponder this, she catches me looking at her blouse, smiles and undoes a button, which arouses me. Deep down I know I should probably do as Justine advised and steer clear of her. Clearly, she is trouble, seeking to manipulate me for her own advantage – but do I mind that? I feel like an emotionally vulnerable serial killer right now. Perhaps I should let her?

'Time to get back to work,' says Faye, picking up her mug and standing up. She leans in towards me to pick up my mug too. Her breasts are now hanging by gravity in front of me, almost entirely exposed at this angle as she lingers there. She must want that promotion pretty badly. What would she do for it? As I rise to my feet next to her, she brushes up against me and whispers in my ear, 'I'll totally fuck you if you recommend me for promotion,' she says.

'Oh,' I say.

'Haha, I knew it,' she says. I blush, which she takes as bashfulness, but it's embarrassment in case anyone can see I'm almost fully erect. I look over at Paul but he's facing the other way and chatting with the politics team. I try to rearrange myself for a moment so that blood flow normalises and the erection passes. It doesn't help that she waits with me.

'I don't know what to say, Faye,' I say eventually when no one is nearby as we walk along the corridor to my office.

'Well, don't say anything,' she laughs, stopping to reach down with her hand. She grabs my crotch and I'm excited by her touch, although it is a bit firm. I alternate my gaze between her lips and her breasts while she still has hold of me. 'Meet me tomorrow after work in the boardroom. No one is ever there after hours,' she says.

'Oh,' I say again, and she laughs.

'Tomorrow at 6 p.m. then,' she says as she releases me from her grip. I nod and she walks away smiling, with a distinctive flick of her hair. I watch her bottom as it disappears into the distance.

For the rest of the afternoon, I sit at my desk distracted; it's been quite a week. I'm not sure whether I like such excitement. I'm normally so careful, but Bella's surprise for me at the hotel has thrown me off. This new excitement from Faye might be helpful as long as I don't overdo it.

Does having sex for favours and potentially killing my rival for a job count as overdoing it – or is it just a well-developed series of coping mechanisms to a severe shock? I do need to find some balance but at least I'm thinking less about Bella, which is positive, although I can't resist checking my phone for messages every forty-five minutes. There aren't any so far today.

Faye would present a completely different prospect to Bella. There's no pretext of an emotional connection or prospect of a future life together with Faye to distract me. This will be a straightforward sex-for-favour transaction between two consenting adults. It could be a win-win, although I suspect HR would not share that view. I think I might even be the victim in this situation – is this how Leighton felt all those years ago with Maxine? Although I suspect the lying bastard was the initiator of that situation.

***

'I'm leaving now,' says Justine.

'No problem,' I shout. It's after 5 p.m. already. I take a quick look at my phone to see if I have any messages, but still nothing.

I spend the next hour at my desk trying to focus on how I might go about killing Terry Peak without any meaningful inspiration. Is it even worth it? If I'd been with Bella I think I might have let him just have the damn job, so in that sense it will be her fault if I kill him. It was her fault Don died – I didn't even particularly dislike poor old Don. Sure, he was incompetent, but largely harmless, at least when he was not being a sex pest. That isn't enough of a reason for him to die or for me to risk detection. So, I rushed and killed him for her. It would be rough luck if it was Don's murder that eventually did for me after such a long and distinguished career as a very discreet serial killer.

Over the next hour sitting at my desk, I almost convince myself that I should just walk away and let Peak have the job, and report Faye to HR for attempted bribery. Then I remember how Peak smirked at me and patted my shoulder with his greasy little hand – he did leave a mark there too when I checked.

'Faye definitely deserves it,' he had said, but it was not to a promotion that he was referring. He's a grubby little man. Based purely on her academic performance, she would only get a mediocre recommendation, so I can see and respect the fact that she would want to improve her chances.

As I ponder the situation, I have a light bulb moment as it dawns on me that maybe I could use Faye and Peak to suit my needs. Both of them would seek to manoeuvre me to their advantage, so why not? My mind moves to my 6 p.m. rendezvous with Faye tomorrow evening and I wonder if it's possible for me to arrange for Peak to be there then too. At the very least they might compromise each other and in a worst-case scenario I could simply kill them both and set it up to look like a murder-suicide. That might perk me up. Not seeing an immediate downside to this plan, I start to think of the practicalities.

The first challenge will be convincing Peak to be in the boardroom at 6 p.m. when no one else is there. I will need a reason for him that he won't share with anyone else. He showed an obvious interest in Faye, so that could be one reason, and he knows she's chasing promotion. A man of his meagre physical appearance is unlikely to get too much attention from hot blondes like her, so I suspect he would jump at the chance to have a private rendezvous with Faye.

I close down my computer and put on my jacket. It's just after 6 p.m. now, so I decide to do a quick sweep of the building; there's no time to waste and only twenty-four hours to prepare before I'm due to meet Faye.

Making my way to the main university entrance lobby I pass the three connecting corridors and each of them are already in darkness. I lie down on the ground and look under the office doors, but I see no sign of lights in any of the rooms. It's safe to assume no one is here. Heading to reception, I see the security guard is there in front of a monitor, although I suspect he's watching porn again rather than CCTV. That's the office gossip anyway and he has that classic pale, dough-like physique of an arch masturbator, so I do believe it to be true.

Reception doesn't look out directly over the board-room staircase but anyone wanting to go there would have to walk right by the main desk. The boardroom is on its own mezzanine floor and the only other way to get there is via the elevator. That's on the other side of reception and as it's only one floor up to the boardroom, it's rarely used, except for disabled access. I could slip up there unseen and so I decide to give it a try. The lift works easily enough and makes only minimal noise, but on arrival at the boardroom I find the door is locked. As PVC for research and based in this building, I have a master key and it unlocks the door without problem. Faye would not have a key and Peak's master key might not work as his will probably only work for his building, not this one. I assume so anyway as my key would not unlock his office door when I tried it in the past. I will need to get there first tomorrow night to make sure it's unlocked.

I let myself in to get my bearings of the room. The lights flick on as I enter; there's a dimmer switch so I'll create suitable mood lighting tomorrow. I use my phone to make a quick 360-degree video of the surroundings to aid my preparations and then inspect the crevices of the corner spaces to remind myself fully of its dimensions. There's a high ceiling with a couple of large exposed beams running across the width of the room, beneath which sits the large Camelot table. That's how it's affectionately known anyway – the VC likes this style of meeting table as a circle apparently provides an equal environment for discussion, although we all know our places in the hierarchy, which defeats the object.

In the corner of the room is a PC connected to a data projector for guest presentations and for video conferencing. I need to engineer an invitation for tomorrow evening from Faye to Peak so decide to try my luck and see if I can guess Faye's log-in details from this machine. Thankfully our university system doesn't restrict log-in attempts in this room in case people get locked out and can't then deliver presentations, so I can have a good few guesses.

Faye's username will certainly be in the same format as my own, so it's only her password I need to figure out. I know her husband is Geoff, so I type in a few variations of his name with no success. Pausing for a moment, I remember they have two kids and I wrack my brain for occasions when I have actually listened to her talk about her personal life. I recall there was a bit of a staff joke that they were narcissists to have named their kids after themselves. I believe they began with G and F – I think it was Georgina and Francis. I try these two, but they don't work either, so I am feeling stumped. I contemplate giving up but then my mind drifts to her peachy bottom walking into the distance and I recall her fondness for CrossFit. That's probably why she has such a nice bottom. I type in 'CrossFit' and this time I don't get an error message. The screen changes and begins to upload her inbox – bingo, I'm in. She really ought to change that.

One thing is obvious to me as I inspect her inbox: she needs to read her emails – there are so many unopened ones. A quick scroll through her unread messages shows me she really is not compliant with our university policy on responding to student messages within three working days. If I wasn't illegally accessing her account, I would have to have a word with her. Is that a sufficient reason to kill her? Probably not, but it's a start. I could work with that; it's certainly evidence of a laissez-faire attitude to her responsibilities and one reason I would have given her a mediocre recommendation.

I'm careful not to leave any obvious digital footprint, so I avoid opening unread messages although some of them look intriguing. But I try to retain focus and instead I compose a new message on her behalf to Terry Peak.

'Dearest Terry…' I write, but that doesn't sound right. She would never write that and he wouldn't believe it. I change the tone and try 'Fancy a fuck,' but he wouldn't believe that either, the fat fuck. So, I need something in the range between 'Dear Terry' and 'Fancy a fuck', which is quite broad – this is hopeless, I have been here too long already.

I type quickly, trying not to overthink it. 'Hi Terry, I couldn't help notice you in the senior common room this morning and thought we shared a moment...' I sit back, smirk and look at the text. This seems to work a bit better, is vaguely plausible, and so I carry on in that tone. Two minutes later I hit send, then delete the message from her sent folder. The message urged him not to reply in case of human resources inspection, but to just meet secretly in the boardroom tomorrow night at 6.30 p.m. I log off and close down the computer. I wonder if he will come?

The Tale of Being Neighbourly

End

Back settled in the UK and driving home from work quietly one night, a track by The Wonder Stuff comes on to the radio and my mind instantly drifts to Jason. It's strange to think that was a year ago and he's no longer playing his music loudly on his driveway, waving his middle finger at people, or offering his opinion on their grass cutting abilities. His body never turned up either – the combination of crocodiles and sharks seem to have taken care of that. But how distressing that must have been for his family. It's a situation that has left me in an oddly reflective mood about my own mortality. And so, I think of a couple of things that have affected me in the last year. Firstly, a work colleague, Malcolm, who I quite liked, died from a stroke. He was roughly my age and had just returned home from a Zumba class, which makes you think. No Zumba for me – he only ever went there to watch, nothing too vigorous, just plain innocent leering at women in Lycra. And secondly, Kamila was due to visit us from Australia and yet did not arrive – she just disappeared.

Malcolm was an athletic guy who I routinely chatted with about our exercise regimes when we stood in the coffee queue at work. He took a cappuccino and I had a latte. We talked about the gym, both stayed in shape, had similar family dynamics and were without question the sharpest dressed males on campus. He liked Ted Baker and I favoured Hugo Boss. Ted Baker suits never quite fit me, mainly because I am so tall. Being six foot four was unhandy when I was a teenager but as an adult it just reinforces my sense of superiority over most of the male population. Malcolm and I shared non-verbal appreciation of how to dress and routinely observed lesser physical specimens around campus wearing an array of terrible clothing choices. This was one of my favourite work pastimes and yet we never really spoke of it, just shared a look. When I heard he'd died I felt a sense of loss for my fashion-aware colleague as so too did some of my colleagues. Although, I'm always suspicious they use that kind of thing as an excuse for a day off – I did notice the weather was good that day.

'How could this have happened to me,' I heard one of them cry on the shoulder of another.

'Yes, it's a terrible thing,' I said as I stood uncomfortably facing two weeping women. That's never my ideal situation.

'I think I might need the day to recover,' said one.

'Of course you do,' I said.

'He was so special to me too,' said the other, crying more heavily now.

'Of course he was. Take the day,' I said, trying my best to get out of the situation as fast as possible.

'Oh, Jez, you are so empathetic, thank you,' they sniffled.

'It's my job, no problem,' I said.

Their faces lit up. I saw one of them gaze up at the sky – not looking to heaven but seeing if the weather would hold up for a day spent in the garden.

Ten other members of my staff took the day off when word got around about this. I wonder how many would need the day off if I had died. None, I expect, but some would take it anyway – kind of like a mourners' bank holiday. My point is that these people are just as bad as me. Higher education is a hotbed of psychopathy, competition, delusion of grandeur and a strong desire to avoid anything resembling hard work.

I remember it was that week where Kamila simply did not show up. I mean she has never shown up – at all. I was certainly anxious about her planned visit and what she might say to upset Maxine, but I had no hand in her disappearance. When Lachlan called two days after she'd been due, I didn't know what to tell him.

'What do you mean she didn't turn up?' he asked.

'I have no idea mate, she's just not here,' I said when he asked. What else could I say? It was true. He was surprised yet relaxed and then panicked twenty-four hours later when there was still no sign of her. The police couldn't shed any light on her whereabouts after she left the airport terminal, and it has stayed that way. Lachlan became frantic about it for the next few months, although the police seem convinced she'd met a new man and simply disappeared. For obvious reasons I didn't believe this. But poor old Lachlan – I guess he loved her after all. His tennis game even went into a downward spiral for months after that. He came over to look for her himself too but couldn't find any trace. The police continued to be no help either; all they knew was that she met someone at the terminal and left as a passenger in a blue Hyundai. The rest was a mystery and yet it had absolutely nothing to do with me.

Lachlan took six months to get over it but now seems better and his place on the club tennis ladder is back to normal. One of his PhD students moved into his house to help him get over his grief. She plays tennis too, so I guess that's working out alright for him. I haven't given Kamila too much thought myself since she disappeared, being more relieved than anything. But as I sit reflecting now, I do wonder what on earth happened to her.

The Present Tale

Tuesday passes slowly at USL and it feels a bit like waiting for Christmas Day. I'm so excited about the evening ahead in the boardroom with Faye and Peak. I'm also now only checking for messages from Bella every couple of hours, which is just as well because it seems she has now completely stopped sending them. In my mind I still see her kneeling in front of her husband and I have to shake the thought away. I suspect that sooner or later I'll need to kill her husband – what was he thinking, waving his erection in my direction. That's not something I will easily get over. He also needed manscaping – women appreciate that.

By 5 p.m. I'm in a state of extreme excitement and need to calm myself down. I contemplate whether to take myself quickly in hand before I meet with Faye so my actions for the evening are not led by sexual tension. Then at least I can think rationally with my head rather than my penis if I need to kill her as well as Peak. There are so many possibilities over how it could go this evening, one of which is even that I don't need to kill either of them. Of course, that's my least favourite option as I really would like to kill Peak if at all possible. I have no motivation to kill Faye, even though she is a very sloppy emailer. She has kids too; I'm not some heartless beast after all. I certainly wouldn't want to kill her before we have sex either.

By 5.30 p.m. I have chosen the theme song to

accompany tonight's activities and have settled on 'They Don't Know' by Tracey Ullman. It is an often-overlooked song, and while Ullman is an average comedienne, she is a surprisingly good singer and nailed this one. The song makes me happy and will give me an excitable yet relaxed rhythm with which to go about my work.

My plan is to meet Faye at 6 p.m. which then gives me thirty minutes before Peak turns up. This is what I have decided to call my 'sex or kill window'. If the situation presents itself favourably we might have sex or else I could simply kill her and frame Peak for it. The other possibility running through my mind is just to entirely wing it and see where it takes me. I can still be ready to step in and bludgeon them as the situation requires, but it could spice things up to experiment a bit and take a chancier approach with an open mind. Trying something different could be a post-Bella form of therapy and aid my recovery. It also gives Faye at least a good chance of coming out of this alive – she may even get that promotion.

It's now 5.45 p.m. and with no one around I open the cupboard in my office and examine the contents of my kill kit. I have the Taser, a couple of knives I've borrowed from the university canteen, two plastic supermarket bags, parcel tape and some hefty rope. I did like the look of the ceiling beams and after examining my 360-degree video clip of the room a few times, I'm fairly sure I could hang the little toad from one of those. I visualise him swinging from a beam with his little legs twitching as if rediscovering his dancing roots before he becomes lifeless. I haven't even hung anyone before, so this is all new ground for me.

At 5.50 p.m. I can sense my heart rate rising as

excitement builds. I hold two fingers to my wrist and count for fifteen seconds, I do the maths in my head and extrapolate it. It's one hundred and forty beats per minute by my reckoning, which is fairly high, noting my resting heart rate is routinely around fifty-two beats per minute. I will need to calm down, so I hum Ullman's song to myself, trying to relax and dial down the excitement, except it seems to stimulate me further, which is unhandy. So I revert to the dreamlike state I felt singing 'White Horses'. This works a treat and I feel myself begin to calm. I pick up my bag and head along the corridor, humming the catchy TV theme to myself.

The corridors are as quiet this evening as they were yesterday. Universities these days – no one around after 5 p.m., it's terrible. The family-friendly policies have a lot to answer for. People use it as an excuse to condense work between 10 a.m. and 3 p.m. when it was really intended to help condense major events or meetings into the middle of the day so parents and carers would not miss out. Now it's used by the lazier element of the academic workforce as an excuse to work short days.

Dancing and humming as I walk, I reach the end of my corridor, look left and right, and there's no one here. Instead of heading right, towards the boardroom, I go left, exit the main building, walking around the back along the concrete path so I re-enter through a door the other side of reception, right by the elevator. Our masturbating security officer is on duty and as I peep around the corner, he doesn't have sight of me. He doesn't look to be jerking off at the moment so maybe that's a myth. I enter the main lobby, quietly pressing the up button on the elevator. A quick check on my phone and I can see it's 5.57 p.m. now so I had better get a move on. The elevator door opens silently and I skip into it, perform a perfect pirouette and now revert back to humming Ullman's tune, happy to be a bit more excited as I get ready for my guests.

As the elevator doors open, I step out of the lift purposefully towards the boardroom. This corridor is dark but my movement triggers the main ceiling strip lighting to turn on, which gives me confidence that I'm the first person here – just as well as it is 5.58 p.m. I'm running a little later than I planned.

I use my master key to unlock the door and enter the room. It's exactly as I left it yesterday apart from a USL mug on the table which appears to contain an apple core. I remove the mug from the table and toss its contents into the bin. I turn the dimmer light down to its lowest setting and this gives the room a sultrier atmosphere, sexy even, and ready for Faye. I place my kill kit behind a stack of spare chairs near the door and take out some basic essential items. I tuck the Taser into the inside left pocket of my jacket so I can draw it out like a gun from a holster. I practise this a couple of times and fantasise about being Clint Eastwood in *Dirty Harry*. I leave everything else in the bag apart from an emergency blunt cutlery knife which I tuck next to the Taser. A quick check of the time again – it's 6.05. but there's no sign of Faye.

I sit propped on the edge of the Camelot table facing the door as I wait for Faye to arrive, although I am beginning to worry she might not show up. It's 6.07. and still there is no sign of her. Peak is joining us at 6.30 and this is not the time for her to be late.

While I face the door, I double check all is in place and run through some likely options in my mind. It's still possible at this stage to simply to leave and forget the whole thing and this makes me think of Bella. I would have given this all up for her and I suddenly feel sad. But with her out of the picture I need this as a distraction and so I refocus on enjoying myself with Faye and Peak.

It's now 6.11. and still there is no sign of Faye. I take a quick look to see if I have any messages from her but there are none to say she has backed out or will be late – there are also none from Bella.

As I start to wonder whether this evening will ever begin, I see the boardroom door cagily open. For a moment I'm unsure who it is and my right hand twitches slightly, ready to draw out the Taser if required. Thankfully I see a head of blonde head hair peering around the door as Faye looks into the room. She's taken her hair out of its ponytail and it looks styled. It's nice she has gone to some effort before we meet.

'Hi,' she says, whispering. She's smiling and doesn't look nervous in the slightest. How many times has she done this?

'Hi,' I say, smiling back, more in relief than through sexual arousal. I relax my right hand away from the Taser. She puts her right index finger to her lips and suddenly she reminds me of Bella. 'Shhhh,' she says quietly as she walks towards me, giggling. She continues laughing gently as she quietly closes in on me, unbuttoning the top of her blouse as she walks. As she gets closer and closer, I see more and more of her plumped-up cleavage. She's not wasting any time, which is good because we really just have a few minutes and I haven't yet decided whether or not I should have sex with her or kill her. Her breasts are almost popping out of her bra, freed from the restricted space of her tight blouse. It can't have been comfortable to wear. Seeing her long hair now loose is exciting and I'm not sure if it's just the lighting but her eyeliner looks darker, sexier and less neutral than usual. She's also wearing a deep red lipstick that exaggerates her full lips, but I am disappointed to see she's wearing trousers. This will make sex much more challenging in the limited time we have available. I was very keen to take her over the boardroom table if time allowed. I think that will be impossible now.

By the time she reaches me her blouse is almost completely undone and beneath it I can see close up she is wearing a tight cream, lacy bra. Her breasts look so swollen as they press heavily on the seams of the bra. She leans in towards me and kisses me. I feel her tongue reach into my mouth as her hand reaches down to my crotch once again. I become hard instantly and I hear her quietly giggle again. She pulls away from our kiss, looks at me and then down to my trousers. Her smile reminds me of Bella and I can't help but think about her for a moment, my true love, and how much I miss her. But then I look at Faye and her magnificent breasts and I forget all about Bella.

Faye is evidently on a tight schedule of her own; she probably needs to get this done before she can get home to tuck her kids into bed. I had better not hold her up. She moves her head to kiss my chest through my shirt. I moan quietly at the softness of her touch and she works her way down my body. She undoes my belt and unbuttons my trousers with only a single finger and thumb. What an expert she is – I would guess she's done this a few times, but I don't mind. She sinks to her knees as she grabs me fully in her hand, looking up into my eyes.

'You're going to like this,' she says and I gulp. She smiles and as I gaze at her, she licks her lips. I bet she watches porn. I quickly glance at the time on my phone next to me on the table. It's 6.18. and Peak will be here imminently, but she is about to take me in her mouth. I really want to let her, but it was only a few minutes ago I was thinking of killing her. Is that wrong? It doesn't seem very romantic, but I guess this is transactional for both of us. Should I let her carry on? My rational brain is struggling with this conundrum and I curse my decision not to relieve my sexual tension beforehand – there just wasn't time. I can't think clearly now and my phone alarm is pre-set to ring at 6.23. I only have a few minutes, but perhaps that might be enough – she looks amazing. So I close my eyes for a moment and lean back against the table.

She glances up at me and I smile back at her before putting my hand on top of her head to encourage her to get on with it as time is pressing on. She laughs as I do so and whips up some speed. What a girl. I glance again at my phone and see the time – it's 6.21. I only have two minutes but that could be enough – should I kill her or climax, kill or climax, and as she works up a furious pace, the decision is made for me and she gulps in surprise.

'Sorry about that,' I say out of politeness. She shrugs, wiping a sleeve across her face – she doesn't look like a hugger and I'm certainly not kissing her now. Just then my phone alarm rings and I fumble to reach it on the table, pretending it's an important incoming call.

'No need to be sorry, just remember this in your recommendation for promotion,' she whispers as she kisses me on the cheek. As I thought, she has terrible breath now as I pull away from her to take the call.

'Sorry – I really need to take this – please just stay as you are and I'll be one minute,' I say. She smiles and shrugs again, thankfully taking out a stick of gum from her pocket.

I do my best to quickly reassemble my trousers as I make a dash for the door. Peak is due in six minutes. I keep the phone pressed to my ear and now pretend to speak quietly to someone on the other end of the call as I exit the room. Once outside I duck down behind the recycling bins in the corridor.

Crouching behind the bins in the darkness of the corridor, I try to catch my breath. Faye had very impressive skills, but I doubt it's something she will be offering to repeat anytime soon, or not until she wants something else. I hope Peak comes soon or else she will be quickly dressed and out of the room.

Thankfully, the corridor strip lighting springs into life and I see Terry Peak strolling towards the boardroom. He's early – I thought he might be eager. He looks even more shifty than usual and as I peer at him from between the bins, I see him straighten his tie, lick his lips, then lick his palms before running them through either side of his balding scalp. He pauses, clears his throat and takes a deep breath before edging towards the door. He looks nervous.

I watch him turn the door handle and disappear into the boardroom. I edge away from the bins to listen outside the door. As I calibrate my hearing to the surroundings, I hear their voices. Peak is speaking animatedly but I can't make out what he says. I can hear Faye responding, her voice slightly louder; it sounds like she is maybe trying to protest and she is definitely trying to speak over him. I contemplate if this is the moment where I should burst in to see what's happening, but I leave it for a few seconds. It's possible, although unlikely, that Faye could get sexy with him too and that could yet be a good outcome. I give it a minute and then I decide to push the door open to see what's happening.

'Is there someone in here?' I say, as I enter the room. Faye is facing Peak and her top is still half undone with her breasts exposed. It looks like she's tried to fasten one of the buttons, but it is sitting awkwardly, so she obviously did it in a rush. His trousers are half undone as he scrambles to fasten his belt.

'What? Wait,' says Peak, sounding a little panicked.

'Oh, I'm sorry, don't mind me. I'm just picking up my USB stick from the computer,' I say, overtly looking away from them, although not before I direct a wink to Faye. I step towards the computer in the corner of the room, taking a USB drive from my pocket and pretending to then retrieve it from the PC.

'Jeremy – I don't know what you think has been going on, but I can assure you…' trails off Peak.

'It's none of my business what you do Terry,' I say. Even in the gloom I can see him redden.

'Faye, please explain this mix-up to Jeremy,' he says pompously. I shoot her a look and thankfully she gets it and joins in, now letting her breasts swing freely. He was an awful letch with her in the coffee room – this is an opportunity for her to give him some payback.

'Oh Terry, tell him the truth,' she says. What a star she is.

'What? No, wait!' says Peak.

'Honestly, it's nothing to do with me Terry, but I imagine David might take a dim view of this kind of behaviour from someone about to take up the role of deputy vice-chancellor,' I say.

'Faye, for God's sake,' says Peak.

'Why did you come here Terry?' she asks him.

'You invited me!' he says, shouting now. 'This is a honey trap!'

'I certainly did not invite you. I have no idea what you are talking about,' she says indignantly, and this is indeed true.

'Well, I really don't need to know what is going on, but I think you probably ought to reflect on this Terry. Faye, I think it perhaps better you come with me,' I say and she nods solemnly, fastening her top. She leaves the room with me while Peak carries on protesting his innocence and buckling his trousers back up.

I walk her to the car park and when we are sure Peak is nowhere to be seen, she grabs hold of me and we share a laugh.

'Oh my god – Peak. What a prick!' she says. Faye's night might be finished now, but as I wave her off, I am thinking of how I need to double back to the boardroom and remove my kill kit before it's discovered.

The Present Tale

It's Wednesday lunchtime and I just got off a phone call from David to say I would be taking over as DVC now that Peak has surprisingly withdrawn.

'I must say it was all very mysterious,' said David. He sounded disappointed, but at the end of the day it had been a decent outcome all round.

'When will you be making the announcement, David?' I asked.

'The VC will do that as a general staff announcement on Friday I believe. So please accept my congratulations, Jez. I'm sure you will do a marvellous job,' he says.

I see Faye later in the coffee queue that afternoon, looking a little sheepish. She's a few positions ahead of me when she sees me. Last night had been a strange one for her. One minute she was with me and then she had Terry Peak exposing himself to her.

'I imagine you have a few questions?' I say, when we have our drinks.

'Yes – but I'm not sure I want to know. Just do that recommendation for me. OK?' she says. I nod.

'So…' I say.

'Yes?'

'Did you pull down his trousers or did he do that himself?' I ask, smiling at her.

'He did! It was horrible – he saw me topless and just

228

dropped them,' she says. I can't control my laughter and thankfully she sees the funny side too. The evening could have turned out so differently.

'How was your morning?' she says, sipping her latte as we walk back to our offices.

'Oh, not anywhere near as interesting as last night,' I say. She stops and stares at me for a moment, sipping her coffee.

'Just so you know, that was definitely a one-time thing,' she says.

'Yes, I know,' I say.

'OK. So, you'll support my application?' she says. I do admire her focus.

'Of course I will,' I say. She nods and I watch her peachy bottom head off towards her office. It was a one-time thing, until the next time – I look forward to it.

Settling back into my office my mind drifts inevitably to Bella. I have hardly thought of her in the last twenty-four hours, but I'll be travelling back home tomorrow. It'll be strange being there, so close to her, and yet no longer being in contact. Perhaps I've been rash – I might reach out to her and see if we can work it out.

Justine pops into the office and places the usual hefty pile of paperwork on my desk. It'll keep me busy for the rest of the afternoon.

As the day draws to a close, I take the decision to drive home to Carlisle early in the morning. My watch is still nowhere to be found, which is completely stressing me out, and I now need to start ruling out possible locations. The first of which is obviously the most critical – Discovery Woods. If it's there and it's ever found with Don's body, then it is all over for me.

Jamie has been messaging me – he's read about a new movie and is excited to go and see it together. So I'll get there in the morning, give myself a few hours to search the woods and then maybe take Jamie to the movie in the evening.

'Goodnight, Jez,' says Justine, jolting me to life. 'Will you be here tomorrow?' I shake my head. It's now time to head back to my flat, pack up some clothes and pick up a shovel ready for the morning in case I need to do some digging. There are still no messages from Bella.

The Present Tale

End

In the morning I drive straight from my flat towards Discovery Woods. Apart from the obvious, everything else has been coming together pretty well. I may not be with Bella any longer but my recent diversion with Faye was fun and it's extremely satisfying that Peak has now been dealt with. It's almost more exhilarating to have him still alive, defeated and working for me now than to have killed him. Just think of all the learning and teaching bullshit I can force on that sycophantic asshole. He'll no doubt be plotting some kind of revenge. For now, I can enjoy that Peak is no longer a threat and as a consequence, I will imminently be confirmed as DVC. This is an excellent and well-earned outcome. As for Faye, repeated sexual performances with her seem unlikely. This feels a shame as she has real potential. If I'm creative, I can probably find a way to convince her into it again. So now I just need to tidy up one loose end – finding my elusive watch.

I make good time on the journey today, there are no hold-ups and as I pull off the main road towards the woods it's still only 11.20 a.m. It's lightly raining, just enough for me to have to put on the windscreen wipers and yet sufficiently damp for most recreational walkers to be put off a trip to the woods. So, I'm feeling blessed with good fortune once again and hopefully all I will need is a quick inspection of the site to rule out that the watch is there and satisfy my mind. I'm dressed casually for the occasion, wearing jeans, walking shoes and a nice light sweater I picked up in an Armani sale. I should blend in well enough if I come across any ramblers.

There are only a couple of vehicles on the side of the road as I enter the county estate and drive up the windy lane towards the small car park backing on to the woods. This is a good sign as dog walkers often leave their cars here. I run through a basic plan of what I will need to do and determine that I should first check my walked route to and from Don's woodland grave. I decide to get into the mood for this occasion as if I were approaching a kill. So, I decide to pop on a jaunty song to get me in a good and bubbly mood for the event – I select 'Male Stripper' by Man 2 Man. It has a good techno rhythm and as I turn up the car stereo system it's fast paced enough to get me bouncing up and down in my seat. It has such a catchy chorus that I think I could even reuse it for my next kill, assuming no ramblers get in my way today and require terminal action.

I turn up the volume again and sing along. If I wanted, I probably still have a decent enough body myself to rock it as a male stripper. Middle-aged women in a nightclub would go crazy for a piece of me.

'I was a male stripper in a go-go bar…' I sing.

'Strip for me babe, strip for you, strip me 'cos I want you to.' This is going perfectly.

I take the last turn of the winding track approaching the car park and suddenly I feel sick. Ahead of me are two police cars with flashing blue and red lights, a police van and a couple of ambulances. One officer is attaching a leash to a menacing-looking dog. I quickly turn off the music system without even completing the last chorus.

I'm not sure what to do. Have I finally run out of luck? I've been pushing it over the years. This is what happens when you rush things. My phone vibrates in my pocket and I'm not sure whether or not to take the call. It's probably Bella begging me to take her back and saying that everything will be OK. I close my eyes wishing that to be the case but fearing it's not. I can't face looking to see who it is, so I let it continue to ring.

I try to gain my composure by breathing deeply and as I do so, I pull the car over into a parking bay furthest from the flashing lights. Think Jez, think and don't panic, I say to myself. But I should panic, why else would there be police and ambulance crews here at this precise location unless they've discovered Don. I think of Jamie and how I have let him down. It will just be him and Maxine now.

I look down to the duffel bag in the footwell next to me and wonder how many police I could take out if I let loose. I could make one last heroic stand like Butch and Sundance. If I am going down, I should at least go down with a bang, one last hurrah to finish things off and cement my legacy as a serial killer of note. It makes me angry that just because of what I do as a hobby, I would have to go to prison for the rest of my life. Other people have done far worse in times of war; my rotten luck it was to be born in peace time. I could have been a great warrior for some army or other. All I needed was a cause; the cause of myself is not something many people will understand.

Feeling ready for action, I grab the shovel and reach into

the bag to take out a trowel. It's hardly a glamorous weapon combination for my last stand but it will have to do. I won't get many of them, but I might at least go out enjoying myself. I turn 'Male Stripper' back up to full volume and let myself slip into its rhythm, clinging more and more tightly to my garden equipment. The phone vibrates again but I just let it go on – whoever it is, it's too late now.

'Strip for me babe, strip for you, strip because I want you to,' I sing as I take a last deep breath, look at my reflection in the rear-view mirror and roar like a lion. I press the door release, swing it open and move to get out. But as I lift myself from the seat, I'm suddenly pushed backwards by someone firmly slamming the door closed back on me. I'm thrust back down into the car by a great force and the door slams shut. I recoil, closing my eyes, adopting a defensive foetal position, shielding myself.

An aggressive voice whispers loudly into my ear. 'Stay the fuck there,' says a woman. But I recognise the voice and as I open my eyes to take a look, I feel a shiver as I'm faced by a banshee, a she-devil staring at me with a maniacal expression, her teeth fully bared.

'Maxine?' I say through the glass of the window.

'Shut up – just get out of here!' she says. The tools I had been holding fall out of my grip.

'Maxine?' I repeat.

'Just go, NOW!' she whispers, tossing something at me. 'And answer your damn phone when I ring!' I nod my compliance to her submissively. I fumble with the key in the ignition, my hand is shaking and it takes me two attempts to get the engine started. Before I do, she has already disappeared as if she were never there.

I wonder for a moment if it's all a dream, but the flashing lights and scurrying activities of the uniformed officers in the car park are not imaginary. But they are not here for me, or at least they have not yet come to arrest me. I sit with the engine running for a moment, watching and trying to make sense of what's happening. There are so many people up here in the car park and as I look towards the ambulances, I see not one but three body bags. Has something else happened here not connected to Don at all? Was that really Maxine or was I hallucinating? I look in the car for what it was she threw at me and then I see it. It's a bit dirty and the face is cracked, but unmistakably it's my Omega Moonwatch. I think again of Maxine's expression and how angry she looked. She didn't look like that when she saw me kill Tommy all those years ago – this was new. She looked more like, like – well, me. Her eyes tore into me like those of a wolf about to pounce on its prey. I look again at the broken glass on the face of my watch – I had left it here, what an idiot. I decide to leave now and drive slowly away from my parking bay, trying not to attract attention. As I pass the emergency vehicles on the way out, I notice a familiar car – it's a Ford Focus. I stop instantly and look at the registration number and my heart sinks. For the first time I also begin to also understand what Leighton was telling me before he died.

I drive slowly back to the house, trying to piece things together. As I pull up in the driveway there's no sign of Maxine's car. It is only just after midday so Jamie will also not yet be home from school. I sit in the car for a few moments, too shaken to immediately get my thoughts together. Before getting out, I look in the mirrors and then through the car windows expecting to see more flashing lights of the police coming for me, but there are none. No one has followed me here.

Inside the house it's eerily silent, everything is in its usual place, most of the washing up has been done apart from Maxine's breakfast bowl and spoon which are in the kitchen sink. I reach into the drinks cabinet, get myself a glass and pour a large whisky. I bring the glass to my nose, savour the smell, knowing this could be my last drink before the police arrive.

I lean on the kitchen table, take a couple more gulps and feel the warmth of the liquid hit the back of my throat. It feels good and I decide to grab the bottle so I can refill the glass at my leisure. Still no one comes to the door, there's no banging, no phone calls, no messages.

I walk from the kitchen, through the dining room towards the living room and pause to pick up my favourite framed picture of Jamie from when he was five years old. He was so cute at that age and this is the one of the two of us swimming on the Great Barrier Reef. In it, he's wearing armbands, grimacing as he clings on top of me, holding my neck and sitting on my chest as I float on my back. He was petrified in case we saw a shark, but he knew that I would protect him at all costs. Putting the picture back down I feel a sensation I can only describe as regret. Not regret for what I have done, as I've enjoyed my life, but I do regret the mess I have left. Maxine retrieved my watch, but what has she done to get it and why was Bella there. I think of calling Bella to see why her car was at the woods and hoping she is alright, dreading what I now fear. I toss back some more whisky and I call her number. There's no answer and so I ring it again. This time there is an answer.

'Yes,' says a female voice. It's not Bella. I think of hanging up but I just stay on the line, silent and unsure of what to do.

'What do you want, Jez?' says the voice. This time I recognise it.

'Where's Bella, Maxine?' I say. There's no answer for a moment. 'Where is she Maxine?' I repeat.

'That bitch is dead,' she says. My head spins and I have to sit down on the ground before I fall.

'What did you do?'

'What I've always done with your bitches!' I put my head between my knees and try to breathe.

'Why would you do that, Maxine?' I say.

'Your little whores shouldn't mess around with a married man. You think I didn't know? You think I don't see you and know you and who you are? I've always known, ever since I saw you kill that homeless guy back in Oxford. I've watched you since then – you've always been mine.'

'In Sheffield you mean, when you saw me with Tommy?'

'No, I came after you that night after I saw you slip away from the pub. You know – that night when you knifed the beggar in Oxford.'

'You saw that?'

'Obviously! It was quite a shock and I didn't know what to do. You left him still breathing and I didn't know what to do.'

'But he was dead.'

'Dead people don't breathe, Jez. After you ran off, I went up to him and he coughed at me. He asked me to help him.'

'So you tried to help him?'

'No silly. I held his nose and covered his mouth. I couldn't let you get in trouble for that. It was then I knew we would be together for ever and you would need me to look out for you.'

'You're very frightening, Maxine.'

'Don't be like that. I've looked out for you all these years, protected you and even now I've done my best for you. We were always fine except for when you messed around with your little whores.'

I don't know what to say any more, all I can think of is Bella, and I feel like my world has ended.

'They will come for us, Maxine. It's all over,' I say.

'Of course it isn't over! I've covered it up again and it will all be alright. Your little whore and her husband will go down for this. Sit tight at the house and wait for me. I have to collect a few things and then we will be on our way.'

'You've killed Bella?' I repeat in shock.

'Shhhh. Don't fret it. It's all taken care of, sweetie. Now it will just be the two of us like it was always meant to be. Just you and me.'

'The two of us?!' I say, but she's hung up.

I suspect the police will come quickly enough; not just for me, but also for Maxine. I don't know how she thinks she has covered my tracks, but if Don is now discovered; sooner or later it will come back to me if I stay here. I realise now I should have listened more carefully to what Leighton was trying to tell me all those years ago when I ended him. '… it was her idea,' he had said. I thought he was being desperate and lying. I should have listened.

Whatever it is she's planning, we can't simply slip away just the two of us – I would never leave Jamie and she should know that.

Turning to walk into the living room I stop suddenly as I see what's on the coffee table. There placed in the middle is a padded envelope and on top of it lies a familiar woman's necklace. I stand still, stunned by Maxine's admissions, then I fill my glass again from the whisky bottle and take another large gulp. This was a present I gave Bella for her birthday last year. I pick up the envelope and rip it open. Inside there's a note and as I pluck it out, I can feel the shape of several small items inside. I read the note:

Some loose ends. Be ready to go when I get back x

It's in Maxine's handwriting – she had obviously prepared for this. I take another drink and turn on the TV while I quietly think to myself. Flicking through the channels I find the local news and I recognise the scene instantly as Discovery Woods. Reading the scrolling news I see that Don had been found in the early hours of the morning, but so too has a husband and wife in a suspected murder-suicide. That must be Bella and Mike.

I shake the envelope to coax the items out. The first thing I see is a passport, it's Kamila's. Poor Kamila, she came all the way over to the UK to profess her love. She must have seen Maxine first at the airport, expecting to sort it all out amicably.

The other item in the envelope is more stubborn to remove and seems caught up in the padded lining, but as I shake the bag, I see what it is. It's a shark tooth necklace. As I see it, I break into a cold sweat and race upstairs.

I spend the rest of the afternoon in Jamie's room, lying next to him, quietly singing and rocking him gently in my arms. I close my eyes and smell the top of his head but his odour has changed now. It's no longer the smell I remember of him as a baby. It's been replaced with a stale and musty stench that I know all too well: it's the smell of death. I try to breathe the air harder to gain even the faintest essence of him, but he feels further and further away from me the harder I try.

I open my eyes for a moment and stare out of his door into the hallway at the suitcases Maxine has packed and prepared for us, ready to leave. My stalker, my wife, my nightmare. I did not see the real her, nor the lengths she would go to, to protect us, just the two of us. But she also did not truly see me, nor I myself and what mattered most to me. I thought I was capable of doing anything to get what I wanted, that I cared for no one and nothing. But I was wrong – I think I might have loved Bella and without question I now know I loved Jamie with all my heart. Perhaps I am not a psychopath after all; I am certainly not a good one.

I hear the front door open and then close. Maxine is back home, but it's too late. As I close my eyes for the last time, I feel cold as blood seeps from my wrists. No song this time, no dance, no excitement. It will soon be all over. Jamie, I'm coming. I hear her walking up the stairs, the sound of a scream, then nothing, just darkness and I'm gone.

About the author

Andrew Edwards was born in Wantage, Oxfordshire and he spent most of his youth in the south of England. He subsequently gained undergraduate, masters and doctoral qualifications at Sheffield Hallam University in Yorkshire before commencing his academic career with the University of Reading in 1999. Since then, he has worked as an academic across the UK, New Zealand and Australia and is the author of the best-selling academic text *Pacing in Sport and Exercise* published by Nova Scientific. He had two young adult novellas published in 2014 and *The Psychopath* is his first adult novel.

Also by Maguire Crime

I

A Breach of Trust

It was the phone call that poisoned everything. It had been long anticipated and dread had taken hold like fungus in a neglected toenail. Maisie meant to hurt me. She'd been planning it for months. My father, when talking about his first wife, slurred that a man knows these things. If she recoils when you reach out to brush her hand, if her eyes drop when you talk up the future, if you discover that your favourite rows – the kind that smash glass and crush plasterboard – have tributaries that flow into small talk, you're in trouble. Beware the unspoken, he said.

Mother, never Mum, says I sound just like him. Until recently that's where the similarities ended. But now I know his pain. I can add it to the long list of things no young person should know. I've been saying nothing for years. You have to do that when your affair's illicit and shameful. Well with that phone call those ugly things were going to be said at last.

'Keir, I'm at the studio. I need to see you. Straight away, please.' Maisie's voice, once honeyed, was tart.

'Sure,' I said, trying to sound strong, 'give me half an hour.' The journey took fifteen minutes but I needed some thinking time. The ascent to the art school is quite a tableau. Few students get to work on the periphery of a cliff face. Perrangyre throws these scenes at you, like fresh bread for the gulls.

Minutes after the call I was plying the coastal path, rehearsing my lines, daring to imagine her replies. I was pre-humiliated, incensed that the succubus on the hill was prepping to lumber me with dead metaphors like sad eyes and a broken heart. As an artist I spend all my time fighting cliché, yet here I was, tailored to wear the very worst.

When I reached the school entrance there was a tramp blocking my way. The wind was up and he seemed to circle with it, like a fart trapped in an eddy. He wore a sandwich board with 'SAVE THE WORLD' emblazoned in red – a dull carmine, old blood. I pushed past him. 'It's too late for that,' I said, 'far too late.'

At the studio doors I hesitated. The coastal wind had violated my hair. I straightened it as best I could. New glasses were removed and stowed.

Maisie was sitting on a paint-flecked table, leaned back and loose. Her arms were stretched behind her. She looked playful. It felt all wrong. I tried to look past the sexual sadism – the morello cherry hair and blush lips she'd contrasted with a virginal-white outfit. But this was Maisie, a tease or nothing. Maybe she feared being nothing. I know I did.

'So, what are we doing here?' I said. This was my self-harming debut and I wanted to do well.

She sighed. 'Keir, c'mon.' She hadn't spoken to me like this since the early days. I was just a boy then. She was a celebrity, the woman who appeared on late night TV and discussed the arts, sometimes making points you could understand; the artist magazines profiled again and again; the self-titled Chair of Artistic Innovation at this sandbox of higher learning. The condescension came naturally. As I'd grown into myself and started to speak up, it tapered off. Now it was back.

'You know what needs to happen,' she said. I swallowed and hoped she hadn't noticed the beads of sweat or the nail canopies, bitten back and splintered. All gooseflesh was safely hidden, draped in a fine suit jacket.

'It doesn't have to happen, does it?' This was maudlin stuff. I'd have dumped me. She fingered her neckline.

'Keir, you're sharp and you pay attention to what goes on around you. That's one of the things I like about you. What other people miss, you get. You've got an old brain. Most twenty-year-olds are impossibly trivial. But not you. So stop pretending. You know it's over. Let's say our goodbyes and part on good terms.'

Maisie was right. I did have an old brain – the kind aged in a barrel. She understood that about me immediately. It's what got me noticed. I looked my years, but behind the eyes she saw sediment – accrued experience. I've never liked my generation. All my heroes are my parents' vintage or dead. Maybe it's envy. My lot are so carefree, aimless and cosseted; the most infantilised iteration of humanity that's ever lived; and in the midst of this gene pool there's me, pissing out, feeling about a hundred years old. My mother jokes I'm living life backwards, so when I'm thirty-five I'll be joyful, and at fifty I'll be bounding up staircases like an idiot, putting on silly voices and pretending to know about things I don't, rather than pretending not to know the things I do.

'I don't think I'm ready,' I said.

'Well I'm sorry but things have moved on,' she said.

'What things?'

'You for a start. You've become a different person.' She was right but this was the first time it had been presented as a problem.

'I'm still me,' I said, which sounded ridiculous then and does now. Maisie's frown confirmed as much.

'You're not the Keir Rothwell of old,' she said, 'you're New Shockley – the artist. Isn't that what you keep telling me? You have a persona. One that's attracting a lot of attention.' At last, I thought, we get to it – the imminent threat of discovery.

'Soon,' she went on, 'you're going to be public property. You'll be judging prizes; you'll be dinner party conversation. When that happens, you won't care about me any more. I know because I had a "me" once.' Wilfully underestimating my feelings was Maisie's neat way of dismissing them. I used to think it would stop as we crept towards parity.

'You haven't changed,' I said, 'more's the pity.' She laughed.

'Keir, we were never going to walk down the aisle together. We had a great time, but it was of the moment. My profile's built since I've been here, there's a lot of people watching my every move. The school wants me to do more. I can't be embarrassed and I don't do fairy tales.' No, I thought, you're more a noir kind of girl.

'I love you,' I said. Maisie's face palsied and I realised that whatever she'd expected me to say, this uncharacteristic grab from the well-rummaged bag of stock platitudes wasn't it. The look of disgust, the creeping surprise, reminded me of Mother's face, the day she found me oiling my length. Odd that I should think of them both.

'I have to go,' she said, getting up. She was halfway to the door when she stopped suddenly, as if she'd forgotten to unlock my manacles.

'Oh, it goes without saying, but this remains our business. There's no statute of limitations on our official secret, understood? If asked, I'll deny it and I'll be believed.'

'The benefit of being a practised liar,' I said. She snorted and was gone.

It didn't take long for me to reach my own studio. Just within the threshold I paused and cast a tearful eye over the work displayed on walls, on tables, on plinths. This was a year's graft, the product of walks with Maisie, workshops with Maisie, pillow talk with Maisie. I circled around the pieces, certain I'd throw up. How empty they looked, how derivative. I reached out to touch the head of a sculpture, a prop in a piece of video art, and felt deep loathing and a pain that began in the gut, quickly rising to the base of my throat. Wherever I looked I saw her – the byproducts of lies and false promise.

I felt disorientated, chemically drunk – a sense of clouding, of burning coal in my sinuses, the return of something old and rotten. I'd forgotten this boy, this precursor to the artist, the kid yet to flirt with civilisation, who now took control where I stood. He ripped the canvases from the wall, tearing, putting a foot through. He tore into towers of copper and plaster; punching, splitting – smashing against chapped pillars until there was nothing left but twisted wireframes and half-picked scabs of hanging bits. A screen cracked and lights left their mooring, strangling fixtures that came loose and fell away.

Finally, myself again and exhausted, I crouched. The

world around me was detritus. I got up and surveyed the damage. Glass crunched underfoot while the waves beyond the window offered a solemn contrast. I had nothing left and was just hours away from having to present these broken wares to an expectant school – the final act in a now fruitless year.

I was going to need a new project, a new reason to be.

MAGUIRE
CRIME

Maguire Crime is an imprint created by
RedDoor Press, in association with Iain Maguire
of High Spirits Press, in which we showcase
the very best in debut British crime fiction. We
select our titles to represent exciting new voices
who push the boundaries of the genre and we
are delighted to share these compelling reads
with you. We hope you enjoy them too.